Blaze

Alaska—the last frontier.

*The nights are long. The days are cold.
And the men are really, really HOT!*

*Can you think of a better excuse
for a trip up north?*

Don't miss the chance to experience some

Alaskan Heat

Jennifer LaBrecque's new sizzling miniseries:

Northern Exposure
(October 2010)

Northern Encounter
(November 2010)

Northern Escape
(December 2010)

Enjoy the adventure!

Blaze™

Dear Reader,

Welcome to Good Riddance, Alaska, a quirky little town in the Alaskan bush where everyone's story isn't quite what it seems. Founded twenty-five years ago by a Southern Belle transplant, Merrilee Danvers Weatherspoon, Good Riddance welcomes an assortment of folks from all walks of life.

Clint Sisnuket is proud of his Alaskan native heritage. The land and his people share an important bond, which is what makes him the best guide in the area. A man of quiet strength whose totem is the eagle, Clint protects the land, his customs and those under his care. Clint deserves a special mate, but what happens when that woman doesn't fit into his world?

I hope you enjoy your stay in Good Riddance. Don't forget to come back next month for a *Northern Escape*.

I always enjoy hearing from readers. Please drop by and visit me at www.jenniferlabrecque.com.

As always...happy reading,

Jennifer LaBrecque

Jennifer LaBrecque

NORTHERN ENCOUNTER

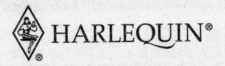

HARLEQUIN®

TORONTO • NEW YORK • LONDON
AMSTERDAM • PARIS • SYDNEY • HAMBURG
STOCKHOLM • ATHENS • TOKYO • MILAN • MADRID
PRAGUE • WARSAW • BUDAPEST • AUCKLAND

Recycling programs
for this product may
not exist in your area.

ISBN-13: 978-0-373-79579-6

NORTHERN ENCOUNTER

Copyright © 2010 by Jennifer LaBrecque

This edition published by arrangement with Harlequin Books S.A.

For questions and comments about the quality of this book please contact us at Customer_eCare@Harlequin.ca.

® and TM are trademarks of the publisher. Trademarks indicated with ® are registered in the United States Patent and Trademark Office, the Canadian Trade Marks Office and in other countries.

www.eHarlequin.com

Printed in U.S.A.

ABOUT THE AUTHOR

After a varied career path that included barbeque-joint waitress, corporate numbers cruncher and bug business maven, Jennifer LaBrecque has found her true calling writing contemporary romance. Named 2001 Notable New Author of the Year and 2002 winner of the prestigious Maggie Award for Excellence, she is also a two-time RITA® Award finalist. Jennifer lives in suburban Atlanta with a Chihuahua who runs the whole show.

Books by Jennifer LaBrecque

HARLEQUIN BLAZE

Don't miss any of our special offers. Write to us at the following address for information on our newest releases.

Harlequin Reader Service
U.S.: 3010 Walden Ave., P.O. Box 1325, Buffalo, NY 14269
Canadian: P.O. Box 609, Fort Erie, Ont. L2A 5X3

1

CLINT SISNUKET LEANED against the window frame in the airstrip office in Good Riddance, Alaska, and watched the snow sifting out of the dark sky.

"Dalton will radio for clearance when he's coming in for landing," said Merrilee Danville Weatherspoon, Good Riddance founder and airfield operator.

Clint turned to her with a slow smile. He liked Merrilee. He'd been pleased when his clan had granted her honorary membership, but there were times she simply didn't understand the native way. But at least Merrilee *respected* the native way, unlike Clint's French-Canadian mother. "I'm not looking for Dalton." The local bush pilot was flying Clint's latest client in from Anchorage. They'd arrive when they arrived. "I'm enjoying the sky."

"Nothing wrong with that," she said. Clint had discovered that people who shared Merrilee's southern origins, liked to talk. A lot. It wasn't unpleasant, simply different. And Merrilee might have spent the past twenty-five years in Alaska, but she still retained her southern roots. Roots were important. They shaped a person, grounded them. "I guess you and Kobuk will see a lot of the sky in the next week."

The malamute raised his head briefly at hearing his name and then dropped his head back on his paws, soaking up the heat of the wood-burning stove across the room. For once Jeb Taylor and Dwight Simmons weren't parked in the rocking chairs that flanked the chess board next to the pot-bellied stove. The two old-timers were pretty much permanent fixtures who argued with each other more than they actually made chess moves.

Clint grinned. "T. S. Bellingham wants to video tape the northern lights, so Kobuk and I will help him." His client was interested in capturing lots of Alaska on videotape, but nothing more so than the beauty of the northern lights, which should be spectacular once the impending storm moved through.

The northern lights, also known as the aurora borealis, fascinated many, Clint among them. His people believed the lights were spirits of ancestors dancing in the sky. He didn't particularly buy that bill of goods but there was a beauty and mystical quality about them impossible to ignore. Even after thirty years, he never tired of them. He knew he never would because the lights were never, ever the same.

"But we won't be seeing the lights tomorrow. Not with this storm blowing in."

Merrilee looked surprised but not skeptical. "I'd better get a weather update," she said, reaching for the radio mic.

It crackled to life before she could pick it up, a disembodied voice announcing through the static an impending storm. They were good for a couple of hours but it was coming. "You sure can call them," Merrilee said to Clint.

Bull Swenson tromped down the stairs. Bull's given name was rumored to be Edward, but Bull suited him much better. Thick and muscular, he had a mane of white hair and a full beard to match. Even in his sixties he could keep up with men half his age. Bull nodded in his direction. "Clint."

"Bull."

The older man looked at Merrilee in obvious affection. "He sure can call what?"

Bull and Merrilee had been an item ever since they'd met. It was well-known throughout town that Bull occasionally asked her to marry him and she routinely turned him down. Apparently a bad first marriage could do that to a person.

Merrilee poured a mug of coffee and handed it to Bull. "There's a storm coming in."

"I could've told you that. My knee and shoulder are killing me."

"You want a couple of ibuprofen?" Merrilee was

already reaching for the bottle on the shelf above her desk before she finished speaking. Clint wondered what it would be like to have someone in his life who anticipated his needs, his responses, that way. If his grandmother had anything to say about it, Ellie Lightfoot was that someone. Clint, however, didn't feel a connection with Ellie, although that made no sense. A schoolteacher from a neighboring village, Ellie was native, beautiful, accomplished and even-tempered—all the hallmarks of a good mate. He'd tried, but he simply couldn't seem to work up any real enthusiasm around seeing her.

"Sure." Bull winced and rubbed at his shoulder. "Damn Viet Cong."

Bull flew a black-and-white POW flag from his front porch. His knee and shoulder aches were, as he put it, "courtesy of his stay in the Hanoi Hilton" during the Vietnam War.

"Here, take these." Merrilee handed Bull a couple of orange pills. "Looks as if there'll be at least half a day's delay in that video Clint's going to help shoot."

Bull shook his head. "It's the craziest thing I ever heard. This Bellingham fella is making a video about Alaska but it's not a documentary. It's just scenery with music?"

"I thought it was sort of crazy myself," Merrilee said, "but I ordered one of his beach videos and it's nice." A faint yearning flickered in her eyes. "Much as I love Alaska, I do miss the Redneck Riviera."

"Redneck Riviera?" Clint asked.

She laughed. "Gulf Shores in Alabama—some of the prettiest white-sand beaches with clear blue water you'll ever see. My family used to go there every summer when I was a girl." Her voice carried more than a hint of nostalgia. "That ambient video's about the next best thing to being there."

"Maybe we should go this summer," Bull said, gruff and abrupt as ever.

She shot a surprised look at Bull. "We couldn't possibly leave in the summer. That's the busiest time of year for both our businesses. This isn't just an airstrip office, remember, it's a bed and breakfast, too."

Bull shrugged. "Neither one of us is getting any younger. If you miss the beach that much, we should go."

"That's sweet, but I'm fine with just my video."

Bull swallowed a mouthful of the steaming coffee. "Maybe those videos of Bellingham's aren't so crazy after all."

Clint nodded. "I haven't seen one but they're a good way to share places and things with people who can't get there. He wants to shoot footage of everything he can while he's here. Northern lights, wildlife, glaciers, footage of snow falling—a little bit of everything. Tomorrow we're going to fly up and stay at the fishing cabin for a few nights. He wants to shoot the lights and we should be able to get some wolf and bird footage there as well." He and Bellingham had exchanged a number of detailed emails. Bellingham had been very clear and straight-forward about his taping objectives. In turn, Clint had made it very clear that it was cold and the cabin was rough, but it was well-situated to view and film the lights. Plus, a wolf pack was known to live in the area. They'd spend the rest of the time at the bed and breakfast which should also afford a good view of the lights from a different perspective while serving as a home base.

"That all sounds good," Merrilee said.

The outing would be respectful of nature and the land, which appealed to Clint.

On the neat and tidy desk, the radio crackled. Dalton Saunders's voice, complete with static, requested permission to land.

The plane's lights appeared as Merrilee granted clearance for the strip. Within a few minutes the small plane was on the ground and Saunders was opening the passenger door for Bellingham. Clint frowned. Not that it much mattered, but he'd figured Bellingham for an average guy. From here, though, it was clear he was far shorter than Saunders and, even in a hooded parka, pretty damn small. This was unexpected, but no problem. Clint didn't mind hauling equipment and Kobuk was a working dog.

Bellingham and Saunders each grabbed a bag and crossed to the airfield door in the glow of the lights reflecting off the white snow.

The second they crossed the threshold Clint felt it—a shift inside him, an inexplicable feeling that passed through his body. It took him a second to realize what he felt was a connection, as if her energy had become his. And it was definitely a *her*—the face framed by the parka's fur-lined hood was decidedly, unmistakably female. She had sparkling spruce-green eyes, pale skin with a smattering of freckles across a straight nose, and a smile that revealed faintly crooked teeth.

Thrown off-kilter by the woman and his reaction to her, Clint did something he seldom did. He spoke without thinking. "Where's Bellingham?"

Saunders was definitely smirking. "Right here."

The woman pulled off her gloves and pushed back her hood. Silky blonde hair fell in a near-white curtain to her shoulders. "I'm T. S. Bellingham." She held out her hand. "You must be Mr. Sisnuket."

Even though he'd never seen her before in his life, a surge of recognition coursed through him. The sense of recognition was so strong, it quite frankly scared the hell out of him. However, he couldn't ignore her outstretched hand. His engulfed hers, and while her skin was warm and soft, her handshake was firm and decisive. Another shock wave coursed through him.

Her eyes widened, her lips parted, and she all but snatched her hand from him. She'd felt it too.

Merrilee launched into her welcoming spiel and Clint shoved his hand into his pocket, definitely thrown off his usual even keel. Dammit, this was what he should've felt with Ellie Lightfoot, one of his kind, not this green-eyed blonde. The last thing he wanted to do was spend nearly a week in *this* woman's company. Five days couldn't end soon enough.

TESSA BELLINGHAM forced herself to focus on the woman speaking to her rather than the man she'd just met.

"Welcome to Good Riddance, Alaska, where you can leave behind what troubles you," said the woman who'd introduced herself as Merrilee Danville Weatherspoon. "Let me hang your coat over here for you." Tessa shrugged out of the down-filled parka and handed it over. Merrilee looked Tessa up and down, her blue eyes sharp but kind. Tessa found the other woman's lace-trimmed pink and gray flannel shirt charming. "And aren't you just a surprise? We all thought you were a man."

Smiling, Tessa nodded. "Sometimes it's easier that way. I've used T.S. on all of my correspondence for years." Single woman, no family—she'd learned early on it was better not to advertise to the world at large she was a female. A little gender confusion wasn't a bad thing. "And when you make arrangements via the internet, whether you're a male or female doesn't usually come up."

"Well, there is that. By the way, I love your beach video."

"I'm glad. That's always nice to hear." A beautiful dark brown dog, with a white face, chest and front legs, and a light brown "mask," crossed the room to sniff at her. The dog didn't look particularly menacing, but neither did he appear overly friendly. No tail wagging accompanied his overture.

"Offer him your hand," Clint Sisnuket said, the first words he'd spoken directly to her. His voice was deep, with a cadence that bespoke his native status. The errant thought occurred to her that she could just close her eyes and listen to him speak…and wouldn't that just throw the whole room yet another curve ball.

He didn't like her—the man, not the dog. Well, the dog might decide he didn't like her either but for sure the man didn't. Actually, dislike was too strong. She was getting an incredible sense of wariness from him. In fact, it was practically rolling off him in waves. Couldn't the rest of the room sense it, too?

"He won't think I'm offering him a snack, will he?" she said with a smile as she held out her hand.

"No, he prefers legs to hands at snack time."

Tessa smiled. At least he had a sense of humor—even if it was a little lame. The dog sniffed her and then startled her when he bumped her hand with his head. "Kobuk likes you," Clint Sisnuket said.

She ran her fingers lightly over the thick fur and scratched him behind his ears. "Hello, Kobuk, you handsome boy." He wagged his upright, curling tail. "You like that, do you? I'm glad *you* like me."

"But then again, Kobuk likes pretty much everyone." Clint Sisnuket managed to make it sound faintly insulting, as if the dog's standards were so low she shouldn't find it remarkable he liked her. It was as if he was trying to deliberately put a distance between them.

She ground her teeth and persisted. "Malamute or husky? I'm not familiar enough with the two breeds to discern the difference."

Wait, had Mr. Stoic/Hostile Native Guide just slipped up and allowed a glimmer of grudging admiration to slip through? "Malamute. He's bigger than a husky."

Merrilee and Dalton Saunders, the bush pilot, finished up their business. She liked Dalton with his sense of humor and easy-going smile, and Tessa had heard all about his fiancée, Dr. Skye Shanahan, on the flight from Anchorage to Good Riddance.

He'd been so obviously in love it had left Tessa wondering what it would be like to have a man feel that way about her—not that she needed anyone. She'd been on her own for so long, pretty much all her life. That's what she knew and that's what felt comfortable. She wasn't so sure she would even know how to have a relationship like that. And the vulnerability...when you cared that much it left you wide open to intense heartbreak. But she'd liked hearing about it.

"Oh, yeah," Merrilee said with a snap of her fingers. "I almost forgot, Dalton. Tell Skye that Gus is covering her on the Thanksgiving dish."

"Will do. Gus is a good woman," he said with a grin.

Gus was a woman? Okay.

"Our Thanksgiving celebration is week after next. The whole town gets together and everyone brings a dish," Merrilee said by way of explanation. "Skye's a good doctor but the girl can't cook. And Skye's busy, so my niece, Gus, is going to make a dish for her. Gus has the bar and restaurant next door—she trained as a chef in Paris."

It was all a little confusing, but most of all it gave Tessa a funny feeling inside to think of the whole town turning out for Thanksgiving. Personally, she'd be just as happy skipping the last half of November and all of December. Family holidays had never been warm fuzzy experiences even though her great-aunt and -uncle had tried.

She'd told herself on more than one occasion she was lucky. Aunt Lucy and Uncle Ted had given her a comfortable home in Tucson when a car accident had claimed both of Tessa's parents when she was in second grade. When the older couple died within a few months of each other after her nineteenth birthday, the house had become hers. She'd always had a roof over her head but there'd been something inherently painful around family holidays.

She came and went as she pleased and answered to no one. Even though she'd grown up in Tucson, she'd never had a true sense of belonging. She'd decided to deem herself a child of the planet, which is what made her so good at finding and videotaping waterfalls and beaches and places that some people would never be lucky enough to see in person. But the holidays…definitely not her favorite time. Oh, sure, Val, who had lived two doors down and become her best friend, and her family always invited her over for Thanksgiving or Christmas but somehow that felt intrusive to her.

However, the notion of the whole town gathering to celebrate intrigued her.

"The whole town really gets together?"

"Well, those who want to. The biggest problem is finding room for everyone, but we manage. This time next year our new community center will be ready. In fact, it should be finished next month. Too bad you're not going to be here then. Of course, listen to me, you probably already have plans." Yep, Tessa had plans. She'd be ordering take-out and editing the footage she'd shot while she was here. Merrilee charged on. "How about a cup of coffee or some hot tea? Or Gus's bar is next door if you need something stronger."

Tessa returned the other woman's smile. "Thanks but something stronger would knock me right out. Hot tea would be lovely."

Dalton finished his coffee and looked at Clint. "That mutt of yours ready to work? Clive's generator came in. And with the storm coming in he may need it. It's sitting on the back of the plane."

Clint grinned and Tessa was totally unprepared for the sheer impact. He looked over at the dog and said, "Work, Kobuk?"

The dog lit up. Tessa could've sworn he offered a canine smile. He shot to his feet and pranced around the room.

"My mutt's ready," Clint said with another of those lethal grins.

"Can you lend a hand, Bull?" Dalton asked.

"No problem."

Clint paused at the door, looking over his shoulder at Tessa. His endlessly dark eyes sent a shiver through her. "We'll go over the week's plan when I get back. This shouldn't take long."

She smiled, determined to get past his wariness. "I'll be here."

The three men and the dog went out into the cold and dark. Merrilee turned to her. "I don't know how much you know about them but malamutes are a working breed. Some of the tourists passing through don't understand it. They think it's cruel, but that dog is happiest when he's pulling a load on a sleigh. That's how they'll deliver Clive's generator. About that tea, green or Earl Grey?"

"Earl Grey," Tessa said, crossing to look out the window. On the airstrip, Kobuk had been strapped into traces connected to a sled. The men hauled a large generator out of the plane's cargo hold. Even with the heavy piece of equipment they were lifting, she noted Clint moved with a deliberateness and ease. They settled the generator on the sled's bed.

In the dark twilight outside, snow dusted Clint's dark head. He was a beautiful man in a wholly masculine way, with high, flat cheekbones that bespoke his native heritage, a knee-weakening sensual mouth, and raven-black hair. He was unusually tall for a native and he possessed maddeningly broad shoulders that jump-started things inside her that had no business jump-starting.

Clint chose that moment to look up, his gaze tangling with hers. Even through the window with its cold draft, a sexual heat rolled through her and her thighs grew damp. She looked away, embarrassed. She had the most ridiculous notion that even from the distance, even though she'd only just met him, that Clint knew that he'd turned her on with just a look across a snowy expanse.

"Here's your tea," Merrilee said, handing her a delicate cup and saucer painted with violets.

"Thank you," Tessa said, grateful for the distraction. This was an unwelcome first. In all of her travels with her job, she'd never been sexually attracted before to any of her guides. She'd have to watch herself with Clint Sisnuket. A relationship with him would be extremely unprofessional on her part.

And yet, she'd never had such an immediate response to any man. There was something different about Clint, something that instinctively drew her. She didn't want to do anything stupid.

2

THERE WAS NOTHING sweeter than the feel of the wind and snow blowing as they moved in sync with Kobuk down the street. Clint and Dalton kept pace with the sled which was loaded with the strapped down compressor in the cargo area. Once they'd loaded up the sled, Bull had headed over to Donna's Engine and Motor Repair to check on a snowmobile engine. Clive, who lived just at the other end of Main Street, could help with the unloading.

"You okay?" Dalton asked.

"Sure. Why wouldn't I be?"

"You seemed a little thrown off balance back there when you saw Ms. Bellingham. Guess she wasn't exactly what you were expecting?" Dalton grinned.

To put it lightly—hell, no, she wasn't what he expected. "Nope. I was thinking she was a middle-aged guy but it doesn't really matter. No worries." Clint was a professional. Just because Tessa Bellingham possessed captivating green eyes and a full lower lip didn't change anything. She was a client. Plain and simple.

Dalton nodded and shot Clint an unconvinced look. Clint's father might've made the mistake of falling for a fair-skinned blonde but not Clint. He'd seen the heartbreak that had resulted. Hell, he'd lived the heartbreak. Thanks, but no thanks.

Dinky Monroe, who could've stepped straight out of a photo from the 1800s when prospectors feverishly sought that vein of Alaska gold that would make them rich, waved from the barber chair in the front window of Curl's Taxidermy/Barber Shop/Beauty Salon and Mortuary. Clint offered a two-fingered salute in return.

Since it was off-season for hunters and there was little in the way of taxidermy work, and no one had died lately, Curl had plenty of time for shaves and haircuts. A mortician before he'd made the move to Good Riddance, he also served as the town's undertaker. But considering how few people lived in the area, relatively few died. Upon the occasional death, Curl set up folding chairs in a back room if a viewing was requested.

"Did you hear Dinky's got a new wife coming in next week?" Dalton said.

Clint laughed and shook his head. "Yeah. My grandmother mentioned it at dinner the other night."

Internet brides had replaced the mail-order brides from times past.

"Your grandmother's better than a newspaper, isn't she?"

Clint grinned. His grandmother ran their family and pretty much the village. "My grandmother knows what's going on, that's for sure." He knew without a doubt that she'd hear through the grapevine about Tessa Bellingham. Then he'd be in for one of their "talks." The "talks" had started when Clint was seven and had been an ongoing part of his relationship with his grandmother.

The wind had picked up and the snow blew harder. Clint had to really hold Kobuk in check. As far as the dog was concerned, the cold and snow was a perk of the job.

At the other end of Main Street, they hooked a right and made quick work of delivering Clive's generator.

"Okay, let's get back and grab a bite to eat before it gets nasty," Dalton said. "We'll probably have to get a late start tomorrow depending on what the storm does."

"No problem. We'll work around it." As far as Clint was concerned, the less time he spent in an isolated cabin with his client, the better.

WHILE MERRILEE FIELDED A phone call, Tessa crossed to the pot-bellied stove and sipped at the warm tea. It felt good going down.

She studied the big open room. It was certainly different from the southwestern style she was used to. Here, the wood walls, ceiling and scarred but highly polished floor set the tone. Two windows overlooked the airstrip out back while another two windows showcased the street beyond. Flowered flannel curtains trimmed in off-white lace hung at the windows—they matched Merrilee's shirt, she realized.

In the back right corner, a desk held paperwork, the phone, and a radio—apparently command central for Good Riddance airstrip. A large calendar, with notations in colored markers, filled the wall-space to the right of the desk.

The opposite corner held a television with two armchairs and a loveseat scattered around a coffee table. It reminded Tessa of the cozy "reading centers" found in upscale bookstores across the country.

A "Welcome to Good Riddance, AK" sign hung over both the front and back doors. Two padded rocking chairs flanked the pot-bellied stove and another rocker sat before a checker/chess table. From the left front corner, a staircase led to the second floor where she was sure the bedrooms were. Three bistro tables draped in tablecloths that matched the curtains occupied the right corner.

And there were framed photographs—lots and lots of them covering the walls, some in color, some in black and white. Large round braided rugs anchored and defined each section of the room in lieu of walls. Between the bistro tables and the potbellied stove stood a door with "Welcome to Gus's" painted on it. Tessa could hear the muted sound of music, conversation and laughter on the other side.

Her flight out of Tucson had been early this morning...and the layover at LAX had been long. Having gotten her bearings in the room, she sank into the rocker next to the stove's warmth. Her initial excitement at having arrived gave way to a tugging lethargy.

Merrilee ended her call. "Sorry about that. Would you rather eat first or shower first? The bath's upstairs and the food's next door." The older woman's smile was infectious.

"A shower would be wonderful, especially since after tomorrow they'll be in short supply for a few days."

"I hear you. A shower it is, then. Right this way."

Tessa pushed out of the rocking chair and followed Merrilee up the wooden stairs to the second floor. Once again, as with the downstairs, the walls and ceilings were all a light, varnished wood. There was something very soothing about all of the wood.

Merrilee ushered her into a room which she instantly fell in love with. A quilt in shades of lavenders, pinks, and yellows covered a queen-size bed. The simple nightstand and dresser were topped with crocheted doilies. Lace-trimmed flannel curtains hung at the windows. A faint aroma of lavender scented the air.

Tessa smoothed her fingers over the obviously hand-made quilt, memories surfacing. "I love it. It's warm and cozy without being fussy." It reminded her of the bedroom her parents had shared.

"Thank you. That's what I was aiming for." Merrilee looked about her in obvious satisfaction. "It just got an overhaul. The roof caved in last month and I figured while we were doing repairs we'd do a little mini-makeover."

"Well, it's simply lovely. I'll enjoy staying here tonight."

Merrilee beamed. "Wonderful. Now, the bathroom is communal and it's at the end of the hall."

"Communal works, especially considering there won't be any running water tomorrow night." Tessa laughed. "I've had quite some experiences in my travels."

Merrilee peered at her from perfectly arched brows. "How'd you get started in this business? It's sort of an unusual occupation."

Tessa knew she had one of the coolest jobs ever filming and putting together ambient videos. Granted she wasn't performing brain surgery but she'd like to think that what she did made a positive difference in people's lives. Whether it was a video of sunrises over beaches or waterfalls from around the world, she hoped it brought the viewer a feeling of calm and peace and the opportunity to see something they might not otherwise see or experience.

"It was just a lucky break. I answered an internet ad and found out I liked all the travel and I was good at it." Tessa smiled and shrugged. "The rest, as they say, is history."

"Do you ever get tired of the travel?" Merrilee perched on the edge of a small armchair upholstered in a sunny yellow fabric with pink accent piping.

Tessa settled on the bed, feeling at ease with this woman she'd just met. Perhaps it was because the room had evoked childhood memories or it may have just been that Merrilee reminded Tessa of her mother. Whatever it was, she felt a connection with this woman she experienced with few others.

"Sometimes—" she paused "—even though I have a place in Tucson, it's never really felt like home. Do you know what I mean?" She probably just sounded like a nut but there was a flicker of recognition and acknowledgment in the other woman's eyes.

"Honey, I grew up in the south and I obviously still have a lot of the south in me, but I never really felt like I belonged there. When I landed here in my motor home, I just knew it was the oddest thing— this was it. This was home." Her smile was full of reminiscence and affection. "Although there wasn't jack all here at the time."

Tessa found herself nodding in acknowledgement. "That's it exactly. I almost feel as if I'm on a quest."

She smiled past the tug of melancholy. "I figure with all of this travel, sooner or later I'll find where I belong. And if not, well, I'll just continue to be a child of the planet, huh?"

Tessa could tell the other woman totally got her.

"Are your folks in Tucson?"

"No. They died when I was eight and I moved to Tucson to live with my mom's aunt and uncle." She'd learned over the years that brevity worked best when talking about her parents, because the sad tale always made other people uncomfortable. "It was a long time ago."

"I'm sorry. Losing parents is never easy. I was fifty when I lost mine and it still was difficult."

For some crazy reason, Tessa almost choked up. She simply nodded.

"Is there a boyfriend waiting back in Tucson?" Merrilee asked, obviously respecting her wishes not to discuss her parents' deaths.

"No. Most of them can't handle the travel and it's just easier to keep strong attachments out of relationships." It had hurt too much when she'd lost her parents and then Aunt Lucy and Uncle Ted had died within months of each other. She never wanted to experience that depth of loss again. Ever. She didn't even allow herself to become attached to a pet.

Merrilee simply nodded but her gaze was shrewd and understanding. Tessa looked away, feeling almost embarrassed by how much of herself she'd just revealed. "I think I'm ready for that shower," she said, bringing the conversation back to less personal issues. Not that showering wasn't personal, but it certainly wasn't soul revealing.

"One hot shower coming right up," Merrilee said as she pushed to her feet.

CLINT FOLLOWED DALTON back into the airstrip office, stopping by the door to clean Kobuk's paws. In an example of weird timing, Bull showed up right behind them. The aroma of fresh-brewed coffee and the fire's heat offered a welcome from the dark cold outside.

Merrilee looked up from where she sat at her desk, filling out paperwork. "Grab a cup of hot coffee."

"Don't mind if I do," Bull said.

Dalton nodded. "The wind's really picking up out there."

"It came up sudden, but I think it's going to be a doozey," Merrilee said.

Clint scanned the room again but Tessa was nowhere to be found.

"Tessa's upstairs taking advantage of a hot shower," Merrilee said. The woman didn't miss a thing. She turned her attention back to Dalton and the flight schedules.

People took showers all the time. He took showers frequently. But Merrilee's words conjured up an image of Tessa Bellingham he'd rather not have.

He could see her standing beneath the water, head thrown back, water sluicing over her pale nakedness, her silvery blonde hair darkened by the shower's deluge. From the moment she'd slipped out of her parka, he'd been mesmerized by the curve of her hips, the indent of her waist and the fullness of her breasts. She had a ripe woman's figure.

Standing around thinking of Tessa naked in the shower, however, was a bad idea. A very bad idea. And hopefully she wouldn't run the hot water out. He could use a shower himself.

He'd decided to bunk down at the B & B so they could get an early start the following morning. Now, with the storm blowing in, it was just as well. His cabin was quite a ways out of town, and often Merrilee offered him his bed for free when one of the people who'd contracted his guide services stayed the night at her place. Clint always made sure, however, that she wasn't full when he snagged a bed at her place. He didn't want to do her out of a paying customer when she insisted on giving him his room for free. She maintained it was payback because she picked up plenty of business due to his guide service.

Overhead the water stopped. While Merrilee finished up paperwork, he busied himself feeding Kobuk his evening ration and refilling the malamute's water bowl. However, the mundane tasks didn't stop him from imagining the woman upstairs drying off, dragging one of the thick, fluffy towels over her neck and shoulder, down her arms, over her breasts, between her thighs and down her legs. He tried mentally running through the supply list he'd put together for their trip but he still couldn't shake the image of her drying herself.

Exasperated with himself, he pulled out the actual list itself and sat in one of the chairs next to the wood stove. Concentrating still wasn't easy. Within a few minutes Tessa made her way down the stairs. Her hair was beginning to dry to a lighter shade where it swung against the curve of her cheek.

A knot of unwelcome want clenched low in his belly. Free of makeup, her skin was clean and fresh, and her green eyes reminded him of spruce bowers. She crossed the room and sat in the rocking chair next to his. She smelled of soap, shampoo and woman. Clint tried to brush aside the awareness coursing through him. He'd been a guide for a long time. He'd had a huge range of clients, some of whom had been attractive, young women but he'd always maintained a detachment. But from the moment Tessa had walked through the door, his detachment had been shattered and he couldn't seem to piece it back together.

"You wanted to go over our plans for tomorrow?" she asked.

"We need to review your supply list to make sure nothing's been left off."

"I guess there's not exactly a Walmart across the street where we're headed, is there?"

Clint found himself laughing. "There's not even a street."

Her quick smile tugged at him. "Perfect. It sounds as if it's just the place I need to film."

"You know there's no running water."

She slanted him an amused glance. "Of course, we discussed it in the email. Mr. Sisnuket—"

"Clint. Everyone calls me Clint."

She dipped her head. "Okay. Clint. I just want to make it clear that I know what I'm getting into. I've traveled to some very remote places under fairly primitive conditions to make my videos. I get it. No electricity. No running water. I'm good with that. All the correspondence we exchanged—that was me. I'm tougher than I obviously must look. I'm not a weak link and I'm not a prima donna. I can hold my own on this trip."

That remained to be seen. "Okay."

"I know you're not convinced—" he wasn't but he didn't think she knew that "—but I'd appreciate you bringing an open mind to this…the whole not judging a book by its cover thing."

He was fairly quick but it took a second for Clint to realize that she'd pretty much just accused him of bigotry. Indignation rolled through him. He'd had his first rancid taste of bigotry at the hands of his mother's family when he'd moved with her to Montreal.

His mother who'd shown up in Good Riddance with a film crew from Montreal. His father should have known better. Should have known the woman from the city with her fair skin and hair would never truly adapt to native life in a small Alaskan village. His father should've known, but he'd listened to his heart rather than his head, and against his family and tribe's wishes, he'd married Georgina Wallace. A year later Clint had been born.

When Clint was five his mother had thrown in the towel on her marriage and living in the Alaskan wilds and moved back to Montreal. It had been a horrible experience for Clint. He missed his father and his extended family, especially his cousin Nelson, who was almost as close as a brother to him, as well as the lifestyle. It hadn't helped that his mother's family thought she'd married beneath her, and they certainly hadn't welcomed a half-breed child who looked full native.

And as if he hadn't learned his lesson well enough, when he'd gone to college at the University of Alaska, he'd been involved with Carrie, a blue-eyed blonde who'd eventually told him she could never get serious with him since she couldn't deal with having mixed race children.

So, if Tessa wanted to know what it was like to be judged by her looks alone, he could tell her about that all day long. He opened his mouth to say just that… and then snapped it shut. She was right.

He'd been perfectly comfortable with taking T. S. Bellingham on this trip. Through their correspondence, he'd ascertained T.S. was competent and knew precisely what to expect from the trip. However, he'd taken one look at the curvy blonde with the delicate features and decided she was going to be problematic and incompetent. Not only had he displayed bigoted behavior, he'd brought his own set of prejudices with him and found her lacking without even giving her a chance.

This time when he opened his mouth, he offered an apology. "You're right. I'm sorry about that. I've definitely been on the receiving end. I suppose sometimes it's easy to see in others what's so difficult to spot in ourselves."

She smiled. Pure. Spontaneous. Lovely. And his heart responded of its own accord, soaring like the mighty eagle, his animal totem, his animal brother.

"Wow. You really are a rare breed of man, Clint Sisnuket."

"How's that?"

Her smile pushed his soaring to new heights. "You're a man...and you just apologized."

Unfortunately for him, he was all too aware of just how much of a man he was...and just how much of a woman he was sitting next to. Soaring was a very bad idea.

3

WHILE THE OTHERS CHATTED to one another in the airstrip office, Merrilee pushed her glasses to the bridge of her nose and tried to relax. She'd been as nervous as a cat on a hot tin roof ever since she'd gotten that stupid letter postmarked from Georgia three and a half weeks ago. *"It's been a long time. We have things we need to talk about. I'm ready to give you what you want."* The words were practically burned into her brain. The only thing she wanted from him at this point was an obituary notice—his.

"Penny for them," Bull said, interrupting her reverie. He gave her a long scrutinizing look from his sherry-colored eyes. That had been the first thing she'd noticed when she met Bull Swenson twenty-five years ago. Her grandmother had kept sherry on her sideboard in a cut-crystal decanter. As a child, Merrilee had thought nothing was prettier than when the sun's rays turned the liquid to molten golden brown.

When she'd first gazed into Bull's eyes, and it had been like staring at sun-lit sherry. In that instant, she'd been done for.

Now anxiety tightened her chest. Bull meant everything to her. What would happen if he found out that she hadn't been honest with him? How would he react if he found out part of their relationship was predicated on a lie?

She forced a laugh. "Just a penny? No way. You'll have to ante up more than that. I may be easy, but Merrilee Weatherspoon is not cheap, sir."

Bull laughed along with her but there was a watchfulness about his weathered face that told her that he knew her well enough to sense her unrest. Luckily the two-way radio chose that moment to crackle to life.

She gave the transmission a go ahead and then couldn't believe what she heard. Dalton and Bull stared open-mouthed. She asked for a repeat. Nope they'd all heard right. Despite the impending storm, a plane was enroute from Anchorage, requesting permission to land at Good Riddance. Someone was in for a rough ride. And though they were booked slap-dab full at the bed and breakfast, there was no way she could refuse an incoming plane landing in light of the storm. She radioed back an affirmative.

She looked at Bull, Dalton, Clint and Tessa Bellingham.

Bull quirked a speculative eyebrow. "Someone's either crazy as a shithouse rat or desperate."

"Maybe both. I hope whoever is flying that plane charged double—" Dalton glanced out the window at the wind kicking up a dust storm of snow "—make that triple."

"It's Durden," Merrilee said, identifying the pilot by the information in the landing request.

Clint nodded. "Durden's a little bit of both. And he'll have to stay over too."

Dalton leaned against the edge of the desk. "Yep. Nobody will be flying out in this tonight."

Merrilee forced a smile. "Good thing we keep extra sleeping bags on hand." She glanced over at Bull. "And if need be I can bunk over at your place."

"Anytime. All the time," he said. She and Bull had always maintained separate residences. It just seemed to work better that way even though she knew he wished they shared the same roof all the time. He'd asked her to marry him more times than she could shake a stick at.

Bull was a good man. Even though she'd fallen for him hard the first time she'd met him, she'd spent the next several years waiting to discover that beneath it all, he was a jerk, that ultimately he'd let her down. Twenty-five years later, she'd finally accepted he wouldn't let her down. Far from being a jerk, he'd proved himself a man of integrity. When Bull gave his word on something, you could count on it. In Bull's book, a man was only as good as his word.

"Y'all might as well head on over to Gus's and grab some dinner while I wait on these fools to show up," Merrilee said. As much as anything, she needed some time alone. "No need in everyone being hungry."

"I'll bring you a plate over," Bull said. "You hungry for anything in particular?"

"Whatever today's special is will be fine." She actually had no appetite but that would simply have Bull scrutinizing her more closely since she hardly ever missed a meal.

"I'll be back in a few."

Clint, Tessa, Dalton and Bull used the pass-thru door, giving her a few minutes alone.

Merrilee gnawed at the inside of her cheek. Sometimes when the truth went untold, the longer it lay there the deeper it became buried.

But now the skeletons in Merrilee's closet were beginning to rattle and she didn't like it a bit. Not even a little.

Tessa looked around her, drawn in by all of the noise, scents and general good fun. They'd walked through the adjoining doors between the airfield and the eatery and Tessa instantly loved it. She was totally digging the old-fashioned bar, complete with brass footstand, lined with an assortment of customers, most of them rugged and a bit rough around the edges. Booths and tables fought for floor space with pool tables, a small stage and a dart board. It was somewhere between a throw-down bar and an upscale diner which meant it defied definition. That made her like it all the more. Uniqueness drew her like nothing else did.

Dean Martin crooned over a speaker system and the smells coming from the kitchen were heavenly.

Tessa was terrible at guessing ages, but a woman who appeared to be in her mid to late-twenties approached, a welcoming smile on her face. With her dark hair accented by one bold streak of white in front, she wasn't so much pretty as she was striking. She extended a hand, "Hi. Welcome, I'm Gus."

Tessa took the woman's hand. "Pleased to meet you. I'm Tessa Bellingham." Gus had a nice, firm handshake. "It smells great in here." Tessa smiled. "I'm suddenly very aware that lunch was a long time ago." As if to lend credence to her words, her stomach issued a loud growl.

Everyone laughed and Gus said, "So it seems. We'll fix you right up. With the storm coming in we're pretty crowded tonight. Do you mind sharing a table? Skye and Nelson have a big table over near the pool tables."

Skye was the name of Dalton Saunders's fiancée. Tessa would like to meet her. "Table sharing is fine with me. The more the merrier."

Bull spoke up. "Gus, how about you put together

two plates of today's special for me and Merrilee. She's waiting on some idiot to fly in before this storm really hits. I'll keep her company while she's manning the airstrip."

"Give us a second and we can pull that together for you," Gus said. She turned back to the rest of them. "I'll send Teddy over to take your orders."

Gus bustled off in the direction of the open kitchen that overlooked the bar area and dining room. Dalton led the way through the dining room tables, with Clint bringing up the rear. Oddly enough, Tessa was infinitely more aware of Clint behind her than all of the other people in the room. It was as if she was tuned into his energy.

They reached the table and Dalton kissed a pretty woman—his fiancée, Tessa guessed—with pale freckled skin, brilliant blue eyes and striking curly red hair. Skye Shanahan and Dalton Saunders made a cute couple.

The man sitting at the table with Skye had long, black hair pulled into a ponytail at the nape of his neck, and his high cheekbones and skin tone indicated he was a native. Skye introduced him to Tessa as Nelson Sisnuket, Clint's cousin and Skye's assistant. Both Skye and Nelson made Tessa feel welcome and comfortable.

Skye smiled at Tessa across the table. "Unless you have issues with meat or wild game, you really should try the moose ragout. It's great."

Tessa nodded. "The moose ragout it is, then. When I'm someplace new, I like to try the local dishes."

Nelson laughed. "That's about as local as you can get. And the moose is fresh." He shot Skye a teasing look. "It was just delivered yesterday."

A flush of red crawled up Skye's neck and face. Dalton chuckled. Clint offered a slow smile that sent a shiver down her spine.

"The moose came from a fellow who trespassed on Dalton's property," Nelson said, "and worse, he tried to poach Skye, as well. He offered the moose as restitution and Dalton had him send it to Gus."

Dalton grinned and shrugged. "Hey, we eat here often enough. I don't cook, and well, let's just say we're better off with Gus cooking the moose than Skye."

"Watch it, buddy," Skye said with a laugh.

"So, he was going to give you a moose?" Tessa was still stuck on that bit.

Skye rolled her eyes. "I thought it was really weird at first too. Frighteningly, you soon get used to the way things are done in Good Riddance. The town has a way of winding its way into your heart."

"I thought it was me," Dalton said. "Now you're telling me it's really just the town you came back for."

The teasing interplay between the couple was fun and stirred a longing inside Tessa. It made her all the more conscious of Clint, who was sitting to her right.

Nelson shook his head in Tessa's direction. "Good Riddance can have that effect on some people. Gus came four years ago and never did go back to New York."

"Gus is the best thing that ever happened to Good Riddance," Dalton said.

"You are so sleeping on the couch tonight," Skye said.

"Sorry, honey, it's my stomach talking instead of my heart."

Tessa laughed aloud and Dalton shot her a grin. "Just wait. You are in for a treat."

Skye nodded. "Gus trained in Paris."

"Wow. And she wound up here?"

"I told you," Nelson said, "Good Riddance has that effect on people."

"And sometimes the infatuation with wilderness living wears off after a while. Not everyone who decides to move here winds up staying," Clint said. His tone was neutral but there was something about him, the way he held his body, that made her think there was some personal story behind his words.

"No doubt about it, Good Riddance can be an acquired taste," Dalton said.

It was early on but so far Tessa liked what she'd seen of Good Riddance. Clint's arm brushed against hers and an awareness quivered through her. There were some things in Good Riddance she liked more than others, and unfortunately for her peace of mind, the man sitting next to her was at the top of that list.

SWEET JESUS, HAVE MERCY! Merrilee eyed the man in front of her with a mixture of loathing and contempt. It had been twenty-five years since she'd seen him and it still wasn't long enough. Of course, she'd pretty much counted on never seeing his sorry ass again and this was still too soon. However, it appeared to be Theodore Jackson Weatherspoon, better known as Tad, standing in the airstrip office.

At least she was fairly certain it was Tad...or maybe just some very bad approximation thereof. The overhead light glinted off his poorly placed hair plugs, and he'd dyed the whole mess some funky orangish-yellow color she supposed was meant to be a shade of blonde. And that was all set off by his spray-on tan. And while Tad had favored button-down Ralph Lauren paired with khakis, this fool was wearing a graphic T-shirt that had obviously come from one of those mall stores which catered to teens and twenty-somethings. And what was he thinking wearing jeans that hung low on his hips? Better yet, what was he thinking with the twenty-something with the collagen lips and silicon boobs hanging on his arm?

"Wassup, Merrilee?"

"Tad?" She nearly pinched herself to verify this wasn't some crazy nightmare, although she'd blessedly not dreamed of Tad in all the time since she'd left him.

He grinned like the total jackass he was. "Not bad for a fifty-one-year-old, huh?"

"Except you're not fifty-one, ace. You're sixty-three."

The blonde next to Tad pursed her lips in equal parts of displeasure and surprise. "Sixty-three, Daddy?"

"Merrilee's confused, baby doll." Tad patted Baby Doll's hand then turned to Merrilee with what she supposed was intended to be a charming boyish smile. "You never were very good at math, were you, Merry?"

She wanted to instruct him to kiss her lily-white ass but under the circumstances she figured she had to play relatively nice. She did not, however, intend to lie down and roll over. He might have the upper hand, to some extent, but he was still on her turf. "Don't call me Merry."

Before Tad could respond, Bull came through the connecting door from Gus's carrying two plates. She could see him sizing up the newcomers as he crossed the room and placed the plates on the desk. He nodded and introduced himself, offering his hand, "Bull Swenson."

"Tad Weatherspoon," the jackass said, shaking Bull's hand.

Of course he recognized the name, he'd only known about Tad for nearly twenty-five years. Bull slanted a quick glance Merrilee's way before saying to Tad, "Ah, the ex-husband, huh?"

It was Tad's turn to glance at Merrilee. "In the flesh."

"This is Jenna," Tad said, motioning to the woman at his side as if he was presenting a prize ribbon at the county fair.

"I'm his fiancée," Baby Doll, nee Jenna, said, holding out her hand, not to offer a handshake but to flash her three-carat, Princess-cut diamond. Merrilee could still size up a diamond from across the room. Tad had obviously gone for quantity rather than quality as the clarity was poor, but she doubted Baby Doll knew the difference.

"Pleased to meet you, Jenna. Nice ring." Bull, ever the gentleman, despite his rough-around-the-edges appearance, admired the jewelry.

"She wanted bling, so she got bling," Tad said.

Bling? Oh, boy.

"Are you hungry, Jenna, honey?" Merrilee asked, and continued without waiting for the younger woman to respond. "And I bet you could use a drink after what was surely a bumpy ride. Bull, why don't you take Jenna over to Gus's while Tad and I sort out their arrangements for tonight."

It was thin, but it was the best she could do on short order. However, Bull's expression clearly told her she had some explaining to do before the evening ended.

The door had barely closed behind them when she faced Tad. "What do you want?" She had no idea how much time she had with him alone and there was no point in beating around the bush.

"Well, hell, Merry, it's been twenty-five years and that's the best you can do?"

She'd told him not to call her Merry but that darn sure wasn't a hill to die on. She let it slide. "Tad, let's get something straight right up front. If you breathe a word to a single soul here that we're still married, I'll gut you like a bottom-feeding catfish."

"I THINK THAT'S THE BEST meal I ever had," Tessa said, her eyes sparkling, her smile genuine and altogether sexy, as she and Clint made their way through the restaurant.

Unfortunately for Clint, she eclipsed every other woman in the room. "Every meal is that way. Gus knows her way around a kitchen."

Across the room he spotted Bull with a woman who looked as if she'd taken a wrong turn on her way to a day at the spa—not your typical Good Riddance visitor. Glancing up, Bull caught Clint's eye. The other man looked grim—well, a little grimmer than usual.

Clint held the door for Tessa to precede him back into the air strip office. Dinner had been great and it was rather disconcerting how much he'd enjoyed her company. She had fit right in with Skye, Dalton, and Nelson. But he had to admit he was damn curious as to who had flown in with the Barbie over at the bar under these conditions.

As he and Tessa walked into the airstrip office, they were clearly interrupting a conversation between Merrilee and an older man who looked very strange. Merrilee turned to face them, the smile on her face not quite reaching her eyes. "How was dinner?"

At his side, Tessa glanced from Merrilee to the stranger, obviously sensing the same level of tension Clint had. "Great."

"Good, good. Tessa, Clint, this is Tad Weatherspoon. Tad, Clint Sisnuket and Tessa Bellingham. Clint's one of our best local guides and Tessa flew in this afternoon from Tucson. She shoots and produces great ambient videos. In fact I've been enjoying one of her beach videos. It's just like being at Orange Beach down in Alabama."

Weatherspoon? And Merrilee was talking a lot even for Merrilee. Tad Weatherspoon had shaken Merrilee and that was a pretty damn hard thing to do. He'd known Merrilee to be animated and outgoing but for the most part she was unflappable. Except now.

"Pleased to meet you," Tad said with a smile that

revealed obviously over-bleached teeth. "I'm the reason Merry moved to Alaska. When she runs, she runs, wouldn't you say?"

Merrilee offered a tight smile. "A continent apart has proved to be a good plan."

Clint wasn't even sure what to say to any of this. He opted for, "Well, we're all glad she wound up here."

"Yep, Merry always was bossy as hell so having her own town to run is right up her alley. Say, if you're a guide maybe you can show me and Jenna, my fiancée, around some this week. You probably saw her next door." He smirked. "I can't wait to see what Merry's done with the place."

Merrilee jumped in before Clint could respond.

"Clint's booked for the week," Merrilee said. "And I'm sure you don't plan to be here very long."

Clint had the distinct impression a cat and mouse game was being played between Merrilee and her ex-husband. What wasn't clear, however, was who was the mouse and who was the cat.

"We're flexible," Tad said, shrugging and flashing his pearly whites once again. "Then I guess you'll have to line us up with another tour guide...or you can always show us around yourself."

Merrilee forced a smile. "That's not going to work out."

"Who knows, we might decide we like Good Riddance so much we don't want to leave."

Clint glanced at Tessa who was watching the by-play with wide eyes. Things had certainly gotten interesting in Good Riddance in the past three hours.

4

TESSA ROLLED OVER AGAIN and glanced at the bedside clock. After midnight. She was tired. By all accounts and purposes she should already be asleep. Instead she was wide awake and restless.

It was as if everyone she'd met tonight was flowing through her brain and she couldn't stop thinking about them. She traveled frequently and met lots of new people, but she'd never felt as engaged by new acquaintances as she had with the citizens of Good Riddance.

And at the top of the engaging-people heap was Clint Sisnuket who happened to be in the room next door. At least tonight there was a wall between them. Tomorrow night they'd be sharing a single-room cabin. The mere thought set her pulse racing.

She hadn't been prepared for the sheer impact when she met the man. Those dark eyes, the high, flat cheek bones, the beautiful hue of his skin, the glossy darkness of his hair, the rich cadence of his voice all tripped her trigger.

And in return she couldn't figure him out. He'd been almost hostile when she'd first met him, but then a couple of times over dinner, she could've sworn he was as attracted to her as she was to him. And she supposed in the long run none of it mattered because she was simply here to do her job and then move on to the next location.

Feeling thoroughly out of sorts with herself and the fact that she couldn't sleep, she pushed aside the quilt and sheet and climbed out of bed. It was chilly outside the covers but she welcomed the cold. She'd worn thick, wool, hiking socks in bed, and now that she was up, her feet felt warm. In an effort to pack light, she hadn't bothered with pajamas and instead was sleeping in thermal bottoms and top. Wrapping her arms around her middle, she wandered over to the window and looked out.

Outside the wind howled and snow swirled like white confetti being blown out of a machine. It took her a few seconds to realize that no lights lit the single street running through the town's center. She rather liked the way it looked with just the rushing snow. Something she couldn't name shifted inside her.

Without giving it a second thought, she grabbed one of her cameras and started shooting through the window. It would probably never make it to one of her videos but she wanted it for herself because there was something very moving about the place at this moment.

Satisfied with what she'd captured on film, she turned the camera off. As she leaned forward, her warm breath fogged the glass. She smiled at her whimsical impulse to trace her initials there the way she used to in the freezer section of the grocery store when she went shopping with her mother. There was definitely something about this room, this place, that evoked childhood memories, memories from the time before she lost her parents.

Tessa put the camera away and crossed to the door. She cautiously opened it to the landing. Merrilee had given her room to the pilot—Tessa couldn't remember his name—who'd flown in Merrilee's ex-husband and his fiancée. Actually, Tessa was pretty sure Merrilee appreciated having an excuse not to sleep under the same roof with Tad Weatherspoon.

Tessa didn't blame Merrilee at all. Tad left a lot to be desired with his big mouth, hair plugs and spray-on tan. The couple was in the room at the opposite end of the hall.

Moving quietly, Tessa eased her bedroom door closed behind her. She made her way down the hall to the communal bathroom guided by a hall nightlight and one in the bathroom, wincing when one of the floorboards creaked loudly beneath her weight.

She finished her bathroom business and smiled

as she washed her hands in the sink that replicated an old-fashioned wash basin. She liked Merrilee's flannel-and-lace shower curtain. It brought a touch of whimsy and softened all the wood in the room without being overwhelmingly feminine and fussy.

Tessa was returning to her room when Clint opened his door and stepped out.

The hall quite suddenly became very tight quarters since he had obviously rolled out of bed and pulled on just a pair of blue jeans and flannel shirt. His jeans were zipped but his shirt hung open, revealing a broad chest well sculpted with muscle. Like men from many native cultures, he had very little body hair, or at least none she could see on his chest.

Tessa forced herself not to stare in the low lighting but her heart thumped in her chest like a wild thing. She had only thought he was potently sexy before. Now she *knew*.

"Excuse me," she murmured, for lack of anything else to say. Something desperately needed to be said, otherwise she'd probably continue to stare at him like a hungry cat eyeing a tin of sardines. For crying out loud, you'd think she'd never seen a man with his shirt open. She had. Plenty of them, in fact. It was just that none of them had been this man and none of them had looked like he did.

"Trouble sleeping?" he asked in a low tone. The shadowed hallway accentuated the angles and planes of his face, the intensity of his dark eyes.

"A little."

"Merrilee keeps some herbal teas downstairs. I know there's one for sleep. Give me a minute and I'll take you downstairs and fix you up with a cup."

"Okay. I'll wait at the top of the stairs."

He nodded. "I'll be right back."

Tessa settled on the top step, listening to the quiet settling of the building beneath the snow's weight and the relentless wind. The toilet flushed and the sink ran. Tessa rose to her feet when he opened the bathroom door. She looked anywhere but at him as he walked toward her.

"I'll go first," he said, brushing past her. She supposed once a guide, always a guide, even if it was only a tea excursion.

Once downstairs he flipped on a lamp and proceeded to set water to boil on a hotplate. He'd buttoned his shirt but she'd already seen what was underneath and couldn't shake that image. She tried desperately not to stare at the man and instead busied herself checking out the framed pictures on the wall. She hugged herself and absent-mindedly rubbed her hands up and down her arms to ward off the cold.

"If you're chilly, take a seat in the rocker next to the stove," he said. "Merrilee never lets the fire die all the way out. It's too difficult to get going again and it gets pretty cold in here."

She abandoned the photos and sat in the padded rocker closest to the pot-bellied stove. For the first time since they'd come downstairs, she noticed Kobuk curled into a tight ball behind the other rocker, next to the back of the heat source. "It does feel good. The heat, that is."

Tessa hadn't planned on running into him in the hallway and she was terribly aware of the fact that she wasn't wearing a bra. The combination of cold and bare-chested man had her nipples standing at rigid attention. She'd keep her bra on at night for the rest of the trip. She brought her feet up to the rocker's seat and hugged her knees, once again glad she'd packed heavy-duty socks. He was bare-footed. "Aren't you cold?"

He was putting two tea bags in mugs when he glanced over at her, a hint of a smile playing about his lips. "No. It'll be much colder in the cabin where we're staying tomorrow night, and don't forget I have thick native blood."

"So, you're immune to the cold?"

"Certainly not immune but I'm used to it. This is a little different from Tucson, huh?"

There was something intimate about being the only two awake and up in the middle of the night, preparing tea, and inanely discussing the weather. "Just a bit," she said, offering a smile. "Snow is a pretty rare commodity for us there."

"Have you always lived in Tucson?" he asked, pouring the hot water into mugs. He sounded genuinely interested.

"I was actually born in Kentucky but I moved when I was eight."

"Your dad got a job transfer?"

"My parents were killed in a car crash and I went to live with my great-aunt and great-uncle in Tucson." She'd found over the course of the years that the best approach was simply to state what had happened and then change the subject. "What about you? Have you always lived in Good Riddance?"

He walked over, handing her a mug with a steeping tea bag and settled in the rocking chair on the other side of the stove. She was grateful for the space between them, glad he hadn't sat in the chair immediately next to hers. "I spent a couple of years in Montreal as a kid and hated it. And I lived in Fairbanks when I went to college. I didn't hate it there but I was definitely ready to get back to Good Riddance. You either love it or hate it here. Good Riddance isn't a place that evokes ambivalence."

"What was it that you hated about Montreal?" She cradled the mug in her hands, enjoying the warmth. "Was it the city versus wilderness thing?"

"That was a factor, but the thing I really hated was the prejudice." There was intent behind his straightforward gaze.

He crossed his legs at his ankles and she rather inanely noted the nice shape of his bare feet.

"That would be unpleasant. I'm guessing that isn't

a factor here in Good Riddance." She blew on and cautiously sipped the tea. It was hot, but not too hot.

"People here pretty much accept everyone else for who and what they are." His hand engulfed his mug. She noticed he had broad and masculine hands and fingers. They looked powerful, strong, and capable. A shiver slid through her at the thought of him skimming his hands up her arms and cupping her shoulders, pulling her close to him. And those were dangerous thoughts to be entertaining over a cup of tea in the middle of the night.

She strove for a light note. "It sounds like Utopia."

He shrugged, a sensual movement on him. "Utopia to some. God-forsaken to others. We're fairly isolated and the winters are long, cold and dark. The nearest shopping mall is a plane trip away. There's no fast food and night life is pretty limited."

She sensed he was repeating what had been said to him more than once. Tessa would bet a dollar to a donut somewhere along the line a woman had hurt him and it had been over Good Riddance.

"You say that as if it's a bad thing," she said on a teasing note.

He shot her a skeptical look. "You don't think so?"

"I haven't really spent a whole lot of time thinking about it," she said, pausing to seriously consider what it would be like to live without malls and fast food and instant shopping gratification. She thought aloud. "You know, growing up in Tucson and living there now, it's just what I'm used to, but I really don't think I'd miss it."

"Sometimes reality is a different animal to deal with when you start living it."

Even though he sounded neutral, Tessa couldn't shake the sense that Clint had some private ax he was grinding. She was curious and altogether more convinced that it had something to do with a woman in his past. She was equally sure he wasn't about to discuss anything that personal, which was a shame because he intrigued her more than any man she'd met before. Outside of his physical attractiveness, which was pretty potent, she was drawn to him on another level whether she wanted to be or not. And as it stood, that didn't strike her as a particularly good thing.

She shrugged a response to his reality comment. "True enough." She wasn't up for debating the topic. And it wasn't as if it had anything to do with her anyway. She was here for the next five days and then she was off on her merry way.

BULL ROLLED OVER AND wrapped his arm around Merrilee, pulling her tight against him in his king-sized bed. She snuggled against him, resting her arm on his. Bull's beard teased against her neck with a comforting familiarity. Sadie, Bull's rat terrier, lay curled against Merrilee's feet at the foot of the bed.

Outside his snug cabin on the outskirts of town, the wind howled in fury and Merrilee couldn't help but think it portended things to come.

It was here. The moment of reckoning she'd known was inevitable—the question that had loomed unspoken between them all evening, even after they'd gained the privacy of his place. Actually, this had been certain to happen eventually from the day she arrived.

But now they were in bed and sleep wouldn't come to either of them until the air was cleared.

She should pipe up but she simply couldn't. Like a coward, she lay wrapped in his quiet strength, drawing from it, and waited on Bull to ask.

Bull broke the silence. "Why's he here, Merrilee?"

She didn't ask who "he" was. There was no need. Damn him to hell but Tad Weatherspoon was clearly in bed with them now. "We didn't get that far today, Bull." She absently stroked her finger against the back of his forearm, tracing the sinewy muscle there.

He stilled her with a hand to her finger. "Did you know he was coming?"

"I had a feeling—"

He cut her off. "And you didn't think you might want to mention it to me? *Hey, Bull, by the way, I suspect my ex is going to show up out of the blue after twenty-five years."*

She wanted to shrink inside herself at Bull's displeasure but she didn't. This was going to get much worse before it got better and she'd learned long ago that shrinking inside herself didn't do a damn bit of good. "I didn't know for sure. I got a letter from him almost a month ago. He didn't say he was coming, he just said it had been a long time and there were things we needed to discuss."

Bull shifted until he was on his side and she was on her back. She missed his arm around her. Even though the bedroom was dark, she could feel him gazing at her. "You've been divorced twenty-five years. What *things* do you need to discuss after all this time?"

There was no easy lead-in, no easy approach, but she still tried. "Bull...sometimes...things get away from a person." Despite the dark, she looked away from his face to the wall. "They go unsaid and after a while it's as if it's too late to say it."

He cupped her jaw in his hand, gently bringing her face back in his direction. "Merrilee, you know I love you, woman. Now tell me what it is that got away from you. Tell me what that asshole ex-husband of yours has flown all the way up here to discuss with you."

Merrilee drew a deep breath. Somewhere inside she'd known that sooner or later this reckoning would come. There were just some things you couldn't run from.

"I believe Tad came up here because he's finally ready to give me a divorce. He's not my ex-husband. He's my husband."

5

"Fantastic," Tessa breathed, her video rolling, the following afternoon as Dalton Saunders banked the plane to the right, showcasing the rugged mountains beneath them. Sunlight reflected off of the snow-cloaked range.

Earlier this morning it had been difficult to believe it was 8:00 a.m. when it was still dark outside, except for the light cast by the pale orb hanging in the sky.

"It's pretty awesome, isn't it?" Dalton said in her ear through the headset. She'd forgotten she was connected to her pilot when she'd spoken.

She briefly glanced his way, smiling and nodding. "*Awesome* works."

But it was more than simply awesome. She'd traveled to a lot of interesting, beautiful places in her job but this was…she couldn't put her finger on it. Somehow this was different. She always wanted to share the beauty of what she found, which made shooting and splicing together her footage all the more special. But there was something else about the scenery spread below her that eluded her.

Perhaps it was partly because her concentration was fractured. She was terribly aware of Clint Sisnuket sitting in the seat behind her in the plane's cramped quarters. It was as if she was tuned into him and couldn't switch channels. As if she was picking up on some shared vibrational frequency. And it was just point blank annoying. She didn't want to see in her mind's eye his inky black hair framing his face with those sexy cheekbones and those dark eyes. They made her simultaneously wonder what he was thinking while inside she skittered nervously at the mere thought of being privy to his private musings. She didn't want to know that the clean scent of man she kept catching a whiff of was Clint's rather than Dalton's. And she did know, as surely as she knew her own name.

A shiver ran through her and she snuggled deeper still into her parka but it wasn't a shiver borne of the cold or the panoramic wonder spread before her. It was a shiver of reaction to the man sitting behind her.

"We're heading in," Dalton said.

Tessa turned the camera off and packed it into the case. Their landing should go smooth enough but you never knew and she had to protect her equipment. The landing itself was part of the adventure. She'd

never landed on a frozen river or lake in a plane out-
fitted with landing skis.

Within a few minutes they were safely on the
ground and her heart was still thumping hard in her
chest. Dalton killed the engine. "Welcome to your
home away from home," he said with his boyish
smile.

Tessa simply nodded, taking it all in. A small
cabin sat perched atop stilts in the ice. She'd seen
website pictures of the cabin in the summer when it
sat in the middle of the lake, accessible only by float
plane and/or boat. Now the only approach had been
via ski plane or snowmobile. According to Clint and
Dalton, since there was no existing snowmobile trail
and they would've wasted precious time blazing one,
especially with all the snow dumped by the storm,
the ski-outfitted plane had been the most viable and
expedient option. Flying suited her just fine. In fact,
learning to fly a small plane was on her life list she'd
made when she'd lost her aunt and uncle. It had been
like losing a second set of parents in a lifetime and
she'd decided life was short and you had to grab what
you could when you could. She revisited her life list
every January.

As Dalton opened his door and climbed out, frigid
cold rushed in. Behind her the malamute sprang to
his feet. With a laugh that seemed to reach inside
and spread through her, Clint gave the dog the okay
to follow the pilot. There was something inherently

joyful in the dog's movement as he leapt from the plane and took off across the snow.

"Aren't you afraid he might run away?" Tessa asked, realizing it was probably an inane question as the dog was a well-trained working dog.

"No. He knows his boundaries."

She had the sense that Clint had carefully chosen that word to remind her that she too needed to re-member her boundaries. She shook her head slightly to dispel the idea. She had to get over this notion that every word exchanged between them was fraught with nuance and hidden text. From now on, she would take their conversations at face value and nothing more.

Dalton opened her plane door. Tessa slung her camera case strap over her shoulder and climbed out. The first thing that struck her was the utter silence and stillness that heralded a deep and abiding peace-fulness. It was a world of quiet painted in shades of light and dark.

Towering snow-draped spruce.

White ice.

The weak sun.

All of it was in contrast to the dark morning and the moonlight-cast shadows. While it had the poten-tial to be eerie, Tessa found it soothing. Even in the raw cold, a warmth seeped through her to her soul. The hush held a spiritual quality she'd never found in any church or cathedral from the grandest to the most humble.

In the distance, a wolf's howl broke the silence, but there was no menace in the sound. Rather for Tessa it held a note of welcome. She'd always liked wolves and was hoping to see some first-hand, which was in large part why Clint had chosen this location.

Even though Clint watched her with his dark eyes and implacable expression, it was Dalton who asked, "So, what do you think?"

"I think it's wonderful." And she did.

Dalton smiled and she could've sworn Clint relaxed somewhat although he gave no visible sign of any such thing. "Well, c'mon, let's get your stuff checked in here at the local Hilton," Dalton said.

Clint chuckled and Tessa also laughed. "If it's got a roof and solid walls, I'll take it any day."

Together they gathered her equipment and headed to the cabin. Inside it was essentially one large room with two bunk platform beds on one wall and two more on another. The bunks were open to the kitchen, which primarily consisted of a propane fueled hot plate on the counter. Utilitarian. Stark. Three windows afforded views of the outside. Majestic. Awe-inspiring.

Perfect…even if she had to share it with Clint Sisnuket.

THE DISTANT DRONE of Saunders's retreating plane faded, leaving Clint alone in the stillness with Tessa.

He turned to look at her. She stood next to him, her fur-trimmed parka framing her face, highlighting the delicate line of her nose and the pale luminescence of her skin. She wore an expression of awe as her gaze seemed to drink in her surroundings. And although he didn't particularly want to relate to anything about this woman, Clint knew how she felt. There were many who became inured to the beauty and wonder of the wilderness when faced with it day to day, but for Clint, the expression on her face was how he felt anew, every day.

Was this the way his mother had looked when she'd first glimpsed the surrounding area? Had his father felt the same affinity? He'd learn from those lessons and was determined not to repeat the same mistakes.

"We should organize camp," he said. She redirected her attention to him, and it was an effort for him to keep his train of thought with her direct green gaze fixed on him. "We also need to eat so that we're ready to set out while we still have daylight."

"But we just ate before we left Good Riddance."

"And we'll eat again. Your body burns a lot of fuel simply keeping warm out here."

"So, I could possibly freeze five pounds off while I am here," she said with a grin.

"Possibly." He found himself returning her grin. There was something captivating about her that was impossible to ignore, seemingly impossible not to get caught up in. And getting caught up in her would be one big mistake he didn't plan to make. There was only one place that would ultimately lead…disaster. They were from two separate worlds, and while those two worlds might occasionally collide, they could never successfully combine. He'd seen it, lived it firsthand…foolishly more than once. "But not if I can help it. If you want to set up your gear inside, I'll be in as soon as I secure the sled."

Her eyes sparkled. "I can help."

"I don't need any help." He realized that sounded abruptly rude and she was a paying customer. "Thanks, though."

Her good humor remained unshaken. "Okay, then I'll just watch."

"Why would you want to watch?" He was genuinely perplexed.

"So, I'll know how to do it I ever need to." She smiled, etching fine lines around her green eyes. "A person can never know too many things."

The odds that she'd need to know in the future how to secure a sled to a piling were slim, but he'd walk her through it. Within a few minutes it was done. She was a quick study. She'd asked a few questions as to the type of knot he'd used and how the extreme cold would affect the materials.

On an unusual whim, he undid what he'd just done and said, "You try it."

She nodded and he could already see the wheels

turning in her head, taking her through what she needed to do. She did great until it came to the last knot. Her frustration was evident when she couldn't get it right on the third try.

"Here," he said, placing his gloved hands over hers, "it's this way. You wrap it under and over in one smooth movement." Despite the gloves and the cold, he could swear he felt the same jolt he'd experienced when they shook hands. And he'd had to lean in, bringing them closer together in the weak daylight, the smoke of her breath mingling with his.

"Oh, I see," she said as she completed the knot properly and stepped away. "Good. Thank you. Now I can add that to my repertoire of things I know how to do." Her laugh held a nervous note. "Not that I'm likely to need to secure a sled in the wilderness in the foreseeable future," she said in a rush, echoing his earlier thoughts, "but if I do, hey, now I've got it down pat."

"I'd trust you to secure my sled anytime." The second the words left his mouth he wanted to snatch them back. Clint didn't say things like that. He especially didn't say things like that to an attractive female client. "You'll soon be qualified as a wilderness guide assistant at this rate," he said on a far less intimate note, trying to smooth over the gaffe.

"Assistant?" Her smile was pure sass. "I'd want to qualify as the guide. And if you're ever interested in a trip to Venezuela, I can show you which plants are poisonous and which aren't."

It was impossible not to smile at her enthusiasm. "That seems like good stuff to know."

"Trust me, it is."

Venezuela and now Alaska. Obviously she traveled extensively. For Clint, the extent of his travel outside of Alaska had been to Montreal with his mother as a child, and that hadn't been as much travel as it had been an exercise in bad judgment on everyone's part. However, it had shown Clint unequivocally where he belonged and who his people were.

"Okay, then," he said, "I'll bore you to no end with information you may or may not need."

"I'm sure I won't be bored."

Possibly not at first, but by the end of the week she'd be bored and more than ready to return to "civilization." Tessa Bellingham no more had "pioneer spirit" written on her than he had "city boy" stamped on him.

He whistled for Kobuk and the dog tore across the expanse of frozen water, stopping just short of them, his tongue lolling out in a happy pant.

"He loves this, doesn't he?" Tessa asked.

"This is his element. The only time he's happier is when he's working between the leads. Wait until he takes us out later today. Then he'll really be doing what he loves."

"I've seen huskies and malamutes at home and it

always struck me as almost cruel that people would keep what was obviously a dog bred for the cold in such a warm place, regardless of how much they shaved them down."

"It's all a matter of habitat. Mother Earth has a spot for each of us, a spot where we belong, where we flourish whether we're a tree, a plant, an animal, or an individual. When one of them is out of its element or habitat, it can never live up to its true potential."

A shadow seemed to pass over her face. "What if the element is an unknown quantity? What about nomads?"

"I think there's a difference between the element being unknown and being nomadic. A nomad is actually in his element, it just happens to be broad."

Her nod was slow, contemplative. "I suppose." He wasn't sure he'd ever moved into such a philosophical realm with anyone quite as quickly as he had with Tessa. She ended that particular discussion by pasting on a distancing smile and moving farther into the tight space. "Do you have a bunk preference?" she asked, clearly steering the conversation back to the practicalities of setting up camp, which is precisely what he should have done.

"I've had a turn in all of them at one point or another and one's just as hard as the next," he said. "But the two on that wall offer the best view of the night sky. I'd take one of them if I were you."

Without hesitation she tossed her sleeping bag onto

the top bunk. "I always wanted bunk beds when I was a kid. There's something cool about sleeping up above like that," she said, her smile once again blooming with an easiness.

Clint smiled back, caught up in the curve of her lips. "And it's warmer up top. Heat rises."

"There is that."

Clint gestured to where Kobuk had curled up near the door. "He'd be just as happy outside and he'd weather the cold just fine but if he's in here with us, it's one more bit of shared body heat."

And that was a poor choice of phrase on his part because the thought that immediately chased "shared body heat" was of the two of them, him and Tessa—not the dog—wrapped in blankets, sharing skin-against-skin body heat. A flash of something in her eyes led him to believe she'd had the same instant image.

She moistened her lower lip with the tip of her tongue. "Speaking of heat, how do you heat the cabin? Or *do* you heat it?"

"You won't think you're in the tropics but we'll knock the chill off with a propane heater. Since it's just one room and fairly small at that, it gets surprisingly warm in a short time. Here, I'll show you how to connect the canister and turn on the heater. We won't, however, leave it on because of the fumes. I'll also get the wood stove going. That's our primary source of heat once the heater warms it up some."

He spent the next few minutes demonstrating the heater and the short-wave radio that provided emergency contact with Good Riddance. It took all of his effort to concentrate on the task at hand rather than on the contrast of the paleness of her hand against his darker weathered one and the scent of her nearness. He'd never had such a primal reaction to another person.

"You'll want to take off your jacket and a couple of layers, otherwise you'll be too chilly when we go out again."

While the heat worked its way into the corners of the room, Clint dug out their midmorning snack. "Caribou jerky," he said, handing a portion to Tess. "It's pure protein, which is what you'll need to see you through the morning."

She nodded and bit off a chunk, chewing thoughtfully. "Not bad. Actually, it's pretty good."

"Beats the hell out of whale blubber."

"I'll take your word on that."

While she ate, she arranged her equipment on the lower bunk farthest from the heater. "I'd like to avoid too much temperature difference—well, as much as possible, so I'll leave them on the bottom bunk and away from the direct heat."

"That makes sense."

"When we start out, would you show me how to mush? That is what it's called when you give the commands and Kobuk pulls the sled, right? Mushing?"

"Sure. I can do that. You weren't kidding about wanting to be guide-worthy, were you?"

She shrugged and although her mouth curved into a smile, the depths of her spruce-colored eyes held a distant sadness. "You're my guide but if something were to happen to you, and accidents do happen, I need to know how to survive out here on my own. At the end of the day, the only person you can really count on to take care of you, is you."

The fact that her statement seemed to have been borne from experience found a home deep inside him. And she was the last woman he wanted wending her way into him.

6

MERRILEE LOOKED AT the numbers on the ledger page for the third time without really seeing them. Biting back a sigh, she closed the book, her concentration not worth a hill of beans today. Of course, that's what not sleeping all night when your man decided he'd move to the couch did to a woman. Bull's sole response had been to murmur, "I can't sleep with a married woman," before he'd left the bed. She hadn't followed him. She knew him well enough to recognize he needed time and space to process everything. He'd been gone before she came out of his bedroom this morning. Actually, she'd heard him leave around five.

She was jerked out of her morose reverie by the sounds of Tad and Baby Doll coming down the stairs. Even if they weren't the only two upstairs, she'd unfortunately recognize Tad's annoying chuckle anywhere, especially in her own home.

It was past noon but rather than be put out by their late appearance, Merrilee was just grateful she hadn't had to deal with his sorry ass any sooner in the day.

"What's shaking, Merry?" Tad said as they entered the airstrip office. Baby Doll—Merrilee couldn't remember the girl's real name to save her soul—teetered beside him on three-inch heels. She obviously had a death wish if she planned to set foot outside in those heels, but then Tad did have that effect on a woman, she thought darkly.

"Your belly when you came in?"

Tad pretended to wince while Baby Doll giggled. "Your tongue is just as damn sharp as it ever was. Baby Doll wants to get her nails done. Can you hook her up at the salon?"

"Salon?"

"Yeah. You know…massage, hair, nails, all that stuff that floats the female boat."

"Have you had a look around town?"

"It was dark when we got in last night. C'mon, Merry, hook her up."

Merrilee picked up the phone and dialed. "Hey, Curl. You busy this morning?"

"I was just finishing up a caribou head. What can I do you for?"

"Nails?"

"Do I need my dremel?" Curl asked. Curl regularly had to attack some of the men's toe nails with a dremel tool. Bull had been dremeled a time or two.

Merrilee glanced at Baby Doll's long finger nails which were probably in better shape already than any other woman's in Good Riddance. "No. You won't need that."

She mouthed at the other woman, "Polish change?"

Baby Doll nodded enthusiastically.

"Just a polish change."

"Polish change? I don't know about that, Merrilee."

"I have total faith in you, Curl."

"If you say so." Curl, however, sounded unconvinced.

"What time?" she pressed.

"I guess whenever. I'm just finishing up."

"Okey, dokey. I'll send her right over." She hung up the phone and smiled brightly at Baby Doll. "He says come right on over. It's just two doors down and across the street. How about I get Teddy next door to take you down?" Teddy, Gus's second in command, would be more than happy to pop out and deliver the other woman to Curl's.

"That'd be great, as long as I'm not putting anyone out," Baby Doll said. When you got past the fact that she'd been foolish enough to hook up with Tad, the woman seemed decent enough. Sadly, she possessed a touch of naivete that reminded Merrilee of herself back when she, too, had bought into Tad's bill of goods.

"Hon, do you happen to have any other shoes with you?" Merrilee glanced at the red stilettos.

The girl smiled brightly. "Of course, I've got these in black and a tiger stripe print." A sudden frown bisected her forehead. "You don't think the red goes with what I have on?"

"It wasn't so much the color as the heel, hon. There's ice and snow out there."

"Oh." She looked simultaneously lost and crestfallen. "No, this is all I brought."

"What size do you wear?"

It turned out that while Baby Doll was at least six inches taller and thirty pounds lighter than Merrilee, they wore the same shoe size. By the time Teddy came over, Merrilee had hooked Baby Doll up with a pair of mukluks that tickled her fancy. She turned one way and the other, admiring her feet and legs. "These are even cooler than Uggs."

"Glad you like them," Merrilee said and mouthed a thank-you to Teddy.

"Wear my red stilettos while I'm gone since we wear the same size. It's sort of like having a sister you can swap with." Merrilee could've kissed Baby Doll for likening her to her sister rather than her mother. The much younger woman beamed. "I always wanted a sister." She waved her hand, "Go ahead, put on those red heels and strut, sister."

Merrilee couldn't help but smile and wave the girl on to have fun. As the front door closed behind Baby Doll and Teddy, she got down to business with Tad. Jeb and Dwight were parked over by the chess board arguing with each other, but since they were both stone deaf, they might as well not even be there.

"Okay, let's get our business done so you and Baby Doll can get back to Atlanta."

"I'm getting the impression you aren't happy to see me, Merry."

"Eat shit and die" wasn't going to get her very far with Tad. Instead she opted for "Okay, Tad, I'm sure you wanted me to see you've managed to find yourself a young honey. I've seen. Poor thing doesn't know what she's in for, but that's not really my business."

"I thought you'd be happy that I'm finally ready to sign those divorce papers."

They both knew he could've sent them by any number of overnight delivery services but Tad had always been about control and playing games. His refusal to divorce Merrilee all these years because she'd dared to leave him had been nothing more than control and his determination to have the last word.

As always when dealing with Tad, Merrilee found herself falling back into the same old patterns. "Well, that's just fine for you, but it doesn't really matter to me any more whether we're divorced or not. I'm not so sure I'll be signing those papers after all."

THE WIND WHIPPED PAST Tess's face, cold yet invigorating as they followed the path the sled cut through the crusted snow. Ahead of her, lashed into his traces, his canine muscles bunching and expanding as he pulled the sled, Kobuk was a beautiful sight to behold as he broke the trail. She was achingly aware that Clint was beside her, his strong hands guiding both sled and dog.

Though his hands were gloved now, she'd noticed them last night and then again during the cabin set up. Today, in better lighting, she'd seen a scar bisecting the back of his left hand.

She gave herself over to the experience of the moment—the wind against her face, the brush of the fur trim against her cheek, the sheer exhilaration of passing through stands of spruce.

All too soon, Clint gave the command and they glided to a stop at the edge of a clearing. It was perfect. Exactly what she'd wanted. Tessa requested a sheltered setting, plus this was the last area he'd spotted the wolves.

"It's pristine," she said, standing and looking around, seriously awed. This would make beautiful, tranquil footage. She turned to Clint without thinking, driven to share the experience with the only other human being there. "It's as if there's no one else in the world and this place is totally untouched. And the silence is unreal. You and I could be the only two people in the world."

He was standing on the sled's back runners. Their gazes locked and the Universe seemed to stand still, to distill to the two of them in a world of light and dark. And even in the cold, there was a heat between them, a blanket of attraction and desire that enfolded them.

She leaned toward him, drawn. He bent his head. The only sound between them was the breaths they drew and exhaled. Tess wondered if Clint could hear the thudding of her heart against her ribs in the deep quiet. His breath, warm, fragrant with coffee, mingled with hers. It was strangely more intimate than sharing a kiss, that gentle coupling of air that warmed her face and teased against her lips. A rush of heat coursed through her in the wake of a longing that wrapped its way around her soul.

His gloved hand cupped her head, his lips hovered a mere breath from hers. Anticipation was sweet as his lips descended to claim hers. A sudden sharp snap jerked them apart, breaking the spell, ending a kiss that hadn't quite gotten started.

Startled, Tessa jumped, nearly losing her footing. Clint caught her, his gloved hands on her arms, and steadied her. She took a cautious step back, forcing him to let her go. Tessa absolutely couldn't continue to react this way to him. She didn't know what it was about him, but she was intensely, incredibly drawn to him.

"What was that? It sounded like a gunshot." And she sounded dismayingly breathless.

"The tree branches snap and crack from the ice. So does the ice in the rivers and lakes. And because there's no other noise, it always sounds very loud."

"You're telling me."

"Have you ever been to a glacier before?"

"No. I'm looking forward to going."

Dalton was scheduled to fly them the day after tomorrow.

"In the summer, it calves directly into the river. The ice creaks and groans and it sounds like artillery fire going off. Of course you won't get that now, but it's still impressive."

"I'm looking forward to it." She looked around. "But this is just amazing." She busied herself setting up one of the cameras on a tripod. Kobuck had settled down, still in his traces. A wolf howled and the dog's ears pricked up.

"That sounds close."

"It's probably farther than you think. Sound travels. However, with the pack in this general area you may get lucky and wind up with some video footage."

He moved swiftly and efficiently, setting up the small low-profile tent the three of them would share. Filming in such cold weather meant having to periodically switch cameras off. Waiting in the tent meant keeping themselves and the equipment warm. It was going to be tight, close quarters which was good from a keeping warm standpoint, but not so good for her resolve to keep her distance from him, especially in light of that almost-kiss. She'd just never counted on reacting to him this way.

Her option however, was to stand around outside like an idiot and freeze her ass off. Nothing for it but to climb into that tent.

CLINT WATCHED AS Tessa opened the tent flap, his attention caught and held by the curve of her rear visible just below the edge of her parka. He definitely didn't need to be checking out her ass any more than he'd needed to almost kiss her earlier, but he just couldn't seem to help himself. There was a lot to be said for self-control and he needed to find some if he was going to be sequestered in the tent and then that cabin with her.

He released Kobuk from the traces and directed the dog to the tent. Sort of a sad state of affairs when a man had to fall back on his dog as a chaperone, although ostensibly Kobuk was another heat source. Ducking, Clint stepped into the tent and pulled his boots off, placing them on the mat near the front. Melting snow was wet and a wet tent didn't exactly work.

Tess had pulled her gloves off and was rubbing her hands together to warm them.

"Give it a few minutes and it'll heat up in here."

There was a flicker in her eyes and that thing that seemed to dance between them flared once again.

"It's—" her voice was husky and she paused to swallow before continuing "—it's already warmer in here than outside."

He nodded. He was plenty damn hot as of right now. "You'll want to pull your coat off and acclimate or you'll be cold when you go back outside," he said, shucking his jacket.

Sitting cross-legged, she pushed the hood back and unzipped her parka. Static left strands of her pale blonde hair standing up. She shrugged out of her jacket, her sweater clinging to the outline of her breasts as she worked her arms free. Clint swallowed hard and pretended to check the zipper on the tent—looking anywhere was better than looking at her breasts with the cold outlining her nipples against her layers of clothes.

In the close confines of the tent, with the biting cold that numbed his sense of smell no longer a factor, her scent seemed to surround him. No perfume, she didn't strike him as a perfume wearer and he didn't smell any, but she was a mix of shampoo, soap and woman. It was a soft, delicate scent that seemed to fit her. She was obviously resilient and capable, but he'd sensed a softness, a vulnerability about her that was grounded more in his intuition than anything she'd said or done.

She wrapped the camera she'd been carrying inside her parka and placed it in her lap. Kobuk lay curled between them. "Does he like to be patted? Rubbed? Or would he prefer to be left alone?"

"That dog will take any attention you're willing to give him. He's shameless."

She scratched Kobuk behind the ears. "He's not shameless. He's a good boy. And he was beautiful pulling the sled earlier today. Weren't you? You did such a nice job," she said in a crooning, sing-song voice. She buried her hands in his fur, kneading and stroking. There was an inherent sensuality to her movements that tightened Clint's gut. It was far too easy to imagine the slide of her fingers and palms against his bare skin, stroking, kneading. And there was the erotic contrast of her light skin against his darkness. Damn it to hell. He had to think about something other than her touching him or him touching her or the thrust of her nipples and the curve of her lips.

He had never been a man driven by his carnal desires, but it was as if Tessa had awakened a slumbering part of him and damned if he knew what to do about it other than ignore it. He hoped like hell he didn't do something totally stupid and unprofessional like reaching over and burying his hands in the silky strands of her hair while he sampled the feel of her mouth and the taste of her tongue against his.

And to compound matters, even though it would be

unprofessional and even though he knew better than to get involved with someone like her—look where it had gotten his father and then him in college—he had a dangerous instinct based on the way she'd looked at him earlier that she was attracted to him as well.

"How'd you get started making ambient videos?" He threw the question out in desperation. And actually, he was curious. It was an unusual choice of profession.

"It's sort of embarrassing to admit but I kind of just fell into it. I'd always liked to fool around with cameras and photography and then a friend of a friend told me about this job on the internet and voila. I discovered I'm good at it and it's very gratifying to be able to bring faraway places to people they wouldn't have access to otherwise. Most people don't have the luxury of starting their day with a beach-front sunrise but with my videos they can enjoy that every morning." She slanted him a look. "In a way, it's similar to what you do. As a guide you take people places and give them an experience they wouldn't have otherwise. How'd you wind up in the guide business?"

"I realized as a kid just how much I love the land. I was always out fishing or trekking. I started working as a guide in the summers when I was about ten." He shrugged. "I knew all the best spots for fishing and hiking, and tourists were a little surprised that I was just a kid but soon word got out that Clint Sisnuket knew his stuff."

"And I bet they thought you were cute." The minute the words left her mouth a blush crawled across her skin.

"I've posed for plenty of pictures over the years. And yeah, there was that whole little native boy aspect. That really worked best here, though. Cute little native boy doesn't always translate well in other places." Chiefly his grandparents' home. They hadn't cared to cart out the child who was clearly not like them.

"Do you still pose for pictures now?"

He laughed. "Not so much now. My cute phase ended several years ago."

"Well, maybe that's a matter of perspective," she said with a teasing smile.

God help him, she was not making resisting her easy. "I got my degree in land management and I freelance as a native consultant on land use." He was damn proud of that. It was a very coveted position and he tried to fill it wisely. "It pays the bills and I feel as if I'm making a difference in preserving Mother Earth."

"So, do you have to go into an office for that?"

"Thank goodness, no. Cities make me feel as if my brain cells are being stamped out. But I do appreciate technology. Every once in a while Dalton flies me to Anchorage or Juneau for a day or two but for the most part I telecommute from home."

"And where exactly is home?"

"About ten miles outside of Good Riddance. You'd hate it."

Amusement warred with annoyance in her eyes. "How would you possibly know what I would or wouldn't hate?"

"Where do you live?"

"I told you last night I live in Tucson."

"Case in point. You live in a city, not the middle of the wilderness."

"I live in a city because it's easier to travel and I have the supplies I need for my videos."

"There you go."

"There you go nothing. That doesn't prove a thing. Well, except that you're a—"

"Rational man," he said, finishing for her.

She wrinkled her nose at him. "Oddly enough, that's not quite the term that came to mind."

The woman was like a dose of positive energy. "I'm sure it was something equally flattering," he said, laughing at her quick eye roll. What was it about her that made him feel just a smidgen more alive and tuned into himself and everyone else?

"I'm beginning to notice a distinct pattern on your part of being wrong."

He crossed his arms over his chest, grinning like a fool nonetheless. "Is that a fact?"

"It certainly seems to be. But don't worry, you have almost a week to redeem yourself."

Kobuk sat up abruptly, ears alert, ruff standing

up on the back of his neck, and issued a low growl. There was a sudden spattering sound from outside.

Tessa didn't exactly look alarmed, more like concerned. "Uh, what was that?"

In all the years he'd been guiding groups, this had never happened. It was pretty cool and pretty damn funky. Probably one of those once in a lifetime events. A dark stain was spreading down the side of the tent behind Tessa. "I'd say the wolf pack is letting us know we're in their territory. We just got pissed on." He spoke in a low undertone.

"Seriously?" she whispered, glancing over her shoulder.

It was about that time that the unmistakably pungent scent of urine seeped into the confined space. At least the cold mitigated the odor somewhat. "Seriously."

"Whew. I smell it."

"If I were you, I wouldn't lean back or it'll be on your clothes."

"Okay. Thanks. I'd rather not wear wolf pee."

Between them, the malamute tensed even more. "Down, Kobuk." The dog reluctantly dropped to his haunches. "The last thing we need is a pissing contest between him and the pack."

"Yeah. Especially since we're in here with him and in the direct line of fire. So, what do we do now?"

He had to give her credit. Not only was she not hysterical, she seemed to appreciate the situation and she had a sense of humor. Damn. He almost wished she'd opted for hysteria. "We wait for them to leave."

As if on cue, a piercing howl sounded right outside.

Tess startled. "Waiting sounds like a good plan to me."

"I'm usually right."

There was nothing quite like getting in the last word.

7

"I FEEL LIKE A HUMAN popsicle," Tessa said, her fingers numb inside her gloves as they closed the door to the cabin behind them.

"I'll have a fire going in just a minute and it'll knock the chill down."

"Chill?" That was an understatement if she'd ever heard it. "My breath is forming smoke rings…inside the cabin."

"We should've taken extra snacks with us. I was surprised at how long the wolves hung around." He unscrewed the top off of a thermos and poured something into a cup. He passed it to her, "Here. Tomato soup."

She sipped at it. "Nectar of the gods. And it's surprisingly warm."

"A good thermos makes a difference." He selected wood from a stack in the corner and loaded it into the stove. "A little dry spruce to get it going quickly and then the alder will burn nice and hot." He struck a match and held it to the kindling, "You'll be toasty in no time."

"I'll just settle for thawed." Even her smile felt frozen. "I still can't feel my fingers."

"Take off your gloves and put your hands in your armpits." He hesitated and then continued. "Or your crotch. They're the two warmest spots on your body. Just so you know."

"Well, that's an interesting survival skill tip. I'll opt for my armpits this time."

"I think that's a good choice," he said, poking at the fire one last time before closing the stove door.

Good grief. He was dead serious. There was an impish part of her that wanted to ask if his hands were cold and offer up her crotch since her armpits were otherwise occupied. And while the thought might dance through her head, no doubt due to oxygen deprivation compliments of the frigid temperatures, she kept the thought to herself. And actually it almost did as much to warm her up as the fire that was snapping and popping in the stove.

She'd known she was in trouble...well, actually, she'd known she was in trouble from the moment she'd met him. But she'd known she was in seriously dire straits when they were sitting in that tent this afternoon and all she could think about was how much she'd like to kiss him. He had the most tempting mouth she'd ever seen on a man. A full lower lip that just begged to be licked and nibbled.

She sucked in a deep breath. She obviously was in need of additional oxygen.

"Are you okay?"

No. She was not okay because even the extra oxygen wasn't alleviating the desire to back him up against the wall and have her way with his sensual mouth. "I'm fine. How about you?"

That earned her a strange look. "I'm fine. Are you sure you feel all right?"

"No. Not really. Is there some kind of mental condition induced by the cold?"

"Hypothermia. Do you feel drowsy? Confused?"

"Maybe a little confused." Because surely she was confused as hell if the only thing she could think about was kissing Clint Sisnuket.

"Let me check your heart rate," he said, placing his fingers against the underside of her wrist while he watched the second hand on his watch. A frown drew his midnight black eyebrows together. He shook his head. "With hypothermia, the pulse rate slows but your pulse is racing."

No kidding. He was touching her. He was within heart-thudding, hormone-revving striking distance. Of course her pulse was racing.

"Uh-huh."

He let go of her wrist and tested his fingers against

her forehead, her cheek, her neck. "You don't feel clammy," he said.

She was seriously in danger of melting into a puddle at his feet. Surely to God, she wasn't in this alone. She looked into his dark eyes with their thick fringe of lashes and saw what she needed to see. "You feel warm." He brushed his fingers against the line of her jaw. Oh, no, she definitely wasn't alone in this. "What kind of confusion are you suffering?"

She drew another deep breath with no better results than before. "I seem consumed by the need to kiss you."

He tensed, much like the malamute had when it had sensed a threat, but instead of retreating, he winnowed his hands into her hair, testing the strands between his fingertips. "I've had the same bout of confusion. But I think it's a bad idea."

"I'm sure it's a terrible idea." She couldn't help herself. She reached up to trace her finger against the fullness of that lower lip that tormented her. She could barely breathe. "You have the most beautiful mouth I've ever seen on a man."

With a muted groan he lowered his head and she wasn't sure where his breath started and hers ended. And then that incredible mouth was on hers, his lips melding against her own.

Sweet.

Hot.

Arousing.

Again. And again. And one more time. She buried her hands in his thick, dark hair.

She caught the sexy fullness of that lower lip between her teeth and nibbled. With another groan, he probed at her lips with his tongue.

She opened her mouth to him. A firestorm swept through her at the sweep of his tongue into the sensitive recesses of her mouth. "Mmm." She took him deeper into her mouth, her tongue tangling with his.

She strained against his erection, canting her hips, and his hands skimmed beneath her layers of clothes to cup her breasts. There was a franticness that had ignited from the first moment she'd seen him.

Finally they broke apart, and as if he'd come to his senses, he withdrew his hands from beneath her clothes. Tessa leaned her head into the strong column of his throat, his heart pounding against her cheek. "Oh, God…"

She didn't realize she'd spoken aloud until he answered her. "I know," he said, his breath stirring against the top of her head.

He gently but firmly set her away from him. "And that's why that's a bad idea. We're both here to work. You'll go home in a week and I'll stay here and anything else is a bad idea."

"But—"

He stopped her with a finger to her lips. "No. I'm not a casual man," he said. "I never have been. It's just not me. And there's no room for anything but casual given how long you're here, so there's simply no room for anything. And that got way out of hand way too fast. I just couldn't…"

She knew he was right. It sounded right. But it didn't feel right. But she thought about grinding herself against him and felt the heat rise in her face. "Me too…I couldn't…"

They each took a step back from the other, as if knowing if they stayed in that close proximity they were going to be right back where they'd just been… unable to keep their hands off of each other.

"Maybe there's room for friendship," she said.

His hesitation stretched between them, broken only by the snap and crackle of the wood. Finally he said, "We could try for friends."

She nodded, feeling as doubtful as he sounded. She didn't normally want to kiss her friends over and over and over while they got naked together.

ONCE AGAIN, THE SUN had sunk below the horizon, casting the world in shades of black and white. Clint and Tessa had ventured out again earlier for her to film in yet another area. He stoked the cabin's fire. It'd need to burn all night. Actually once he started the fire, he never let it go out completely. It was far easier to rekindle than to start another fire from scratch. And the wood stove wouldn't be the only thing burning all night.

Dammit to hell, he'd known kissing Tessa was a bad idea. No, it wasn't just a bad idea, it was a disaster of an idea. Make that a disaster of epic proportion. All damn afternoon he'd tasted her against his mouth, his tongue. Her scent had seemed imprinted on him, marked as clearly as the alpha wolf had marked their tent earlier. That kiss had ignited a fire in him as surely as when he'd held the match to the kindling. And just as he would keep the wood stove going, Tessa would keep him going. His fire wasn't likely to go out as long as he and she were sharing space.

And he'd better just get the hell over it because he'd meant what he'd said earlier. He wasn't a man given to casual relationships and he'd known better than to begin something with her. But he hadn't just wanted her, the need to kiss her had been a hunger gnawing at his gut. And rather than feeding and satisfying that hunger, it had merely intensified it.

And now here they were, cozied up in the cabin for the night and tomorrow night as well, hoping the aurora borealis made its appearance. And there was no forgetting that kiss. But he'd agreed to aim for "friends" so that was the direction he'd take.

"Are you pleased with the footage you got today?" he asked, putting their dinner on top of the wood stove to heat. Gus supplied her dinners frozen, and with the temperatures being what they were, they stayed frozen on the trip out.

Tessa was skimming the day's taping. She sat

cross-legged on the top bunk opposite the window that would offer the best view of the northern lights.

"I'm very pleased. There's a nice shot with two of the wolves. Hang on a sec and I'll show you." She glanced down at a notepad. "Here, let me back it up to this stop." Remaining seated, she angled the camera with its lens viewer his way. It left Clint with no option except to step closer. Holding the camera, she pushed a button and he watched as a rangy gray wolf and a heavier white-flecked wolf loped across the clearing and dodged into the copse of snow-laden spruce.

It was a beautiful scene. However, Clint was more tuned into the delicate bones of Tessa's wrist, the elegant line of her hand. She was like an ivory carving—pale intricate curves and delicate lines, yet resilient and strong.

"Nice, huh?" she said.

"Very. Lots of people who live in Alaska have never been so lucky as to see that." He stepped away to stir the stew that was beginning to burble on the stove's cast iron ledge, eager to put the cabin's distance between them once more.

"And now lots of people will get to see it. Isn't that cool?" Her smile reflected satisfaction. She clicked the camera off and unfolded her legs, dangling them over the side of the bunk.

"You really love what you do, don't you?"

"I do."

"It means you have to travel a lot, though." He would be miserable. He loved the Alaskan wilderness. He'd hated Montreal. Fairbanks had been better but he'd still been happy to come home. "Do you ever get tired of that?"

She shrugged, a guard sliding into place. "Not really."

"Anyone special waiting at home for you?"

"No. I'm something of a wanderer. I move around pretty often."

"But there's nothing interesting enough to make you want to stay, obviously."

"Obviously not." She jumped off the bunk, landing lightly on her feet. "Wow, dinner smells great. What are we having?"

He followed her lead. Obviously that particular topic was closed. "Gus's caribou stew."

The wood popped and snapped in the stove. Between the fire and the stew and Tessa it felt homey in the cabin. He ladled stew into a melamine bowl and passed it to her. "The spoons are in that cup on the shelf." The cabin, which mostly housed hunters and fishing enthusiasts, didn't have a table. "If you use the edge of the shelf as a table," he said, "you'll have a great view of the night sky."

She took his advice and propped her hip against the window frame and studied the sky while she took a bite of their dinner. "This is better than the finest restaurant I've ever been in."

"What? The food or the view?"

She smiled at him over her shoulder and it felt as if the plank flooring beneath his feet shifted. "Both." She turned back to the window, her expression of awe reflected back in the window. "Do you ever get used to it? Take it for granted?"

"No. Never." Even though he'd only been a kid, his time in Montreal had taught him to never take the place he called home for granted. Right along with the lesson that not everyone would love this place as much as he did.

TESSA BURROWED INTO the sleeping bag thrown onto the top bunk and watched the night sky through the window. Outside, the wolves called to one another with a series of howls. There was an almost comforting element to the sound of the wolves. She issued a sigh of contentment.

Clint spoke up. "You okay? You don't need to worry. The cabin's safe. You're safe."

She had deliberately looked out the window rather than at him. He was in the lower bunk directly across from her. She assumed because it afforded him the closest access for stoking the stove. She didn't want to think about the fact that only seven feet separated them. If she didn't look at him lying in his bunk, then she was less likely to think about what kissing him had been like. She wouldn't think how easy it would be to slip into his bunk with him and touch her lips to his, to run her fingers through his straight, thick hair, to trace his high cheekbones, to slide her fingers down to the penis she'd felt outlined so perfectly between her thighs earlier today.

"The cabin seems perfectly sturdy and the wolves don't scare me. I like to hear them."

"My people tell a legend of the origin of the wolf if you'd like to hear it."

"I'd love to."

There was a soothing cadence and rhythm to Clint's voice as he recounted the folktale. Much as she was enjoying the story, Tessa's eyelids grew heavier and heavier. Her last thought before sleep claimed her was that the cabin would protect her from the wolves but who would protect her from this attraction she had for Clint?

"THAT WAS FUN," TESSA said with a radiant smile as they returned to the cabin the following day. "And I'm starving."

Smiling, Clint hung his coat on the peg by the door and pulled off his snow crusted boots. "Your snack will be served momentarily, madam."

Kobuk waited patiently on the mat at the front door. Clint wiped the snow from his coat and paws with a worn towel.

"It'd better be," she said with a smile as she unwound a bright pink scarf from around her neck.

He'd learned a long time ago that guiding in the winter was much better if he took his clients out for brief periods of time and then brought them back to warm up. This morning they'd headed south, following the river's winding, iced surface while she filmed.

Unlike the previous day which had been quiet and still except for the presence of the wolves, the area they'd found had been busy—or relatively so, as busy as Alaska could be in winter—with an abundance of small chirping chickadees and a few magpies. Tessa had been delighted by the presence of the chickadees. They actually reminded him of her—small, happy, social. And on the way back, they'd seen the wolf pack again.

Humming beneath her breath, she crossed to the bunks on the right and plopped down on the lower platform. She pulled out her cameras and did whatever it was that she did to them. She took meticulous care of them, which he respected. He'd seen far too many people in his years as a guide who were careless with their things. And inevitably those were the people he was glad to say goodbye to by the time they left.

He stood for a moment, watching her, almost transfixed by her hands. Her nails were short, neat and unpainted. He wanted to touch her and be touched by her. He longed to trace the delicate blue vein from the back of her hand to the tender spot of her wrist, to know the texture of her skin.

He turned abruptly to the supplies stored on the kitchen counter. He was hungry for her and she wanted cheese crackers and some dried fruit. This was a helluva time and place for him to develop this crazy attraction. And it was crazy, insane…but very real, very intense nonetheless.

Her footsteps sounded on the cabin's wood floor as she crossed to stand in front of the wood stove, backing her nicely curved rear up to the heat, holding her hands behind to absorb some warmth, as well.

Clint wasn't sure how it happened, unless he was simply careless in his distraction, but as he turned he dropped the dried fruit. Apple rings and banana chips scattered over the floor. "Damn," he said.

They both dropped to the wood that had been worn smooth over the years and began to pick up the pieces. Wasting food out here simply wasn't an option. "I'll eat this," he said, "since it's been on the floor."

She picked up the last piece, returning it to the bowl.

"Heck no, you won't," she said with a smile that turned him inside out. "I've been eyeing these apple rings. A little floor time never hurt anyone." She leaned forward and the curve of her shoulder brushed against his arm. On their hands and knees in front of the wood stove, the only sound the sizzle and pop of the green birch he'd loaded earlier, their eyes met and held and it was as if time hung suspended.

And in that moment everything that had been dancing between them, the furtive looks, the brief touches, the longing that was an almost-palpable force roared to the forefront.

Like the winds that could tear across the open expanses at times, desire and need hurtled through him. And an answering hunger gleamed in her eyes. With mutual groans, they reached for each other. Their kiss was frantic. Her lips seemed to feed on his even as he devoured her mouth with his own. Still on their knees, they pressed against each other, her hands tangled in his hair, and he molded his fingers against the fine bones of her skull, her hair a silken mantle against the backs of his hands.

Her breasts pressed against his chest and blood pooled hot and thick between his legs. Their tongues tangled and she arched against him, sending even more heat spiraling through him. She swallowed his groan as he smoothed his hands over her back, quickly learning the curves he'd admired.

She slid her hands beneath the edge of his shirt, under his thermal top, and the sensation of her fingers against his bare skin was even better than he'd imagined.

"Clint," she said, her breathing as ragged as his own.

His brain fogged with want, he didn't know whether she was asking him to stop or not stop. And he ought to have the internal fortitude to call his own halt, but God help him, if she wanted him, he could no longer deny how much he wanted her, as well.

"Yes…should I…"

"Take off your shirt…please. I spent all last night lying in my bunk…wondering."

He knew, had known from the moment he'd seen her that he didn't need to do this. And there was a part of him that had known from the moment he'd laid eyes on her that this was inevitable. There came points when freewill and destiny and desire crossed paths to only one possible outcome.

What the next outcome would be was yet to be seen, but for now, here, there was only one thing he could do and it wasn't to walk away.

"I will if you will," he said. "Because I too have wondered."

With a slow, sweet smile, she grasped the hem of her shirt and the undershirt beneath it and slowly slid them up and over her head. His mouth went dry and his blood ran hot at the perfection before him—the delicate expanse of her neck, the slope of her shoulder, the curve of her breasts spilling out of the top of a white and pink bra, and the indent of her waist that gave way to the flare of her jeans-clad hips.

"Your turn."

_8_

TESSA TREMBLED IN ANTICIPATION. His dark eyes holding her gaze, Clint pulled off his shirt and tossed it aside. In one smooth movement he took off the thermal undershirt.

Her breath caught in her throat. "I just want to look at you for a moment. You are beautiful."

And he was. It was the upper body of a man who worked and worked out. Broad muscled shoulders, well-defined biceps, a chest that rippled with definition down to a flat belly. All of this covered by possibly the most beautiful expanse of skin she'd ever seen. Due to his native heritage, he was naturally several shades darker than she was, somewhere between the richness of mocha and café au lait. The very sight of his bare chest made her ache and the wetness between her thighs dampened her panties.

She reached out and drew a finger over the ridge of his shoulder to his pectorals. The texture of his smooth warm skin sent a shiver through her. Leaning forward she inhaled his scent and then followed the same path of her finger with her lips and her tongue, kissing his skin, tasting him.

He pulled her to him, his breath stirring against her hair in a sigh. His fingers and his broad palms were warm and arousing as they slid up and down her back in a slow, sensual caress.

Still kneeling, he claimed her lips with his. Although he hadn't spoken a word, there was a reverence in his kiss, in his touch. She felt a sense of wonder at the depth of the kiss, at the feel of his velvet skin over muscles of steel beneath her questing hands. He slid her bra straps down her shoulders and trailed nipping, sucking kisses over her neck, across her chest, her body tightening with each touch.

He licked at the valley between her breasts and she shuddered against his mouth, arching her back, desperate for the touch of his lips and tongue against her intimately. But he continued to nuzzle and suck at the tops of her breasts until she was nearly writhing with the need to have his mouth on her nipple.

"Clint." Ragged with want. Desperate with need.

He made a low, sexy sound in the back of his throat and pushed aside the bra. His tongue toyed with her pearled tip. The sensation arrowed through her, straight to the increasing want between her thighs. She gasped. And then his mouth, wet and warm, suckled her. It was unlike any sensation she'd ever known—it was raw and elemental. Like an animal in the wild, she dug her fingers into the rigid muscles of his shoulder and instinctively threw her head and shoulders back, thrusting her nipple further, harder into his mouth, a mewling sound blossoming low in her throat.

Clint uttered a rich sound of satisfaction that reverberated against her. He took her other nipple into his mouth and worked the same magic while he fondled the other one. Over and over and over until she was nearly mindless with want, he stoked the fire inside of her higher and higher until she felt as if she might explode simply from the hard tug of his mouth on her nipple, the slight nip against her aching tip.

She'd always thought she simply didn't have very sensitive breasts. Obviously, she'd simply never had the right lover. She was teetering on the brink of an orgasm and all he'd done was suckle her. As if he sensed the edge she skirted he stopped, filling his warm, big hands with both of her breasts, his lips trailing back up her neck.

"You are beautiful…and so sensitive." He made that sound of satisfaction low in the back of his throat. "Do you want to move to the bunk or should I bring the sleeping bags down here?"

Thank goodness he didn't have the stupid idea they should stop, because if they didn't finish what they'd started, she really thought she might just expire on the spot from frustration and want.

"On the floor. In front of the stove."

He pulled his sleeping bag down and unzipped it, spreading it in front of the stove. Tessa did the same with hers, throwing it on top of his like a blanket. When she wasn't all wrapped up in kissing and touching, she definitely felt the chill of the cabin. Gooseflesh prickled her exposed skin. Without wasting any time she finished undressing and dove beneath the top sleeping bag, sliding to the spot nearest the wood stove. Hey, he was the Alaskan, used to the cold, not her.

She turned her attention to Clint, just as he pulled off the long johns, which were in no shape, form or fashion remotely sexy. However, the underwear quickly followed and *sexy* just picked up a new definition because she was looking at it. Sweet mercy. He was, bar none, the most beautiful man she'd ever seen naked—not that there'd been a lot before him, but enough for her to know who topped the list when she saw it.

Lean hips framed his penis, which jutted proudly from a thatch of dark hair. Muscular thighs and legs, all in splendid proportion to the rest of his body, gave way to well-shaped feet.

She pulled back the edge of the sleeping bag. "Why don't you climb in? I'd hate for you to catch a cold."

"Honey, with you naked in front of me, I could stand outside and not be cold," he said, sliding beneath the cover and facing her.

"Good answer." She slid her arms around his neck and her body to his, intimately.

She deliberately licked the fullness of his lower lip before kissing him. He groaned and rocked his hips against her, his erection nudging at the wet curls between her thighs.

He trailed his hand down and over her hip, stroking, fondling, his touch sure and firm—a man who knew what he wanted and wanted what he had in front of him.

Tess reached between them, stroking the length of his erection. The hiss of the water sizzling out of the birch wood in the stove next to them seemed to extend and echo his "Oh…"

His cock was heavy and hot in her hand and she touched her thumb against his plumbed tip, finding a pearl of moisture there.

Clint was on his own quest. He delved between her folds, brushing against the part of her that wept with the need for release. Instinctively she guided his cock to her wetness and ground against him.

Tessa had never, ever ached for a man the way she ached for Clint Sisnuket. It wasn't just the manifestation of a physical release—it was *him*.

For one glorious moment, for one spectacular time out of mind, he slid inside her, filled her. Bliss.

And then he withdrew.

What the...

"Protection," he said. "I don't have any protection." He looked positively stricken and in that particular moment Tessa thought that she might just be the other side of smitten with Clint.

She pressed a quick kiss to his forehead and said, "Hold that thought. I don't usually carry condoms but my best friend thought it was funny to slip some into my suitcase."

"Well, go, woman. What are you waiting for?"

There was something spine-tinglingly sexy in the way he called her "woman" that upped the ante for her. Feeling remarkably unselfconscious, she climbed over him and made a quick dash for her suitcase.

Chillbumps covered her. "Oh, my God, it's cold without the sleeping bag and the fire."

"Maybe it's not the sleeping bag or the fire that's keeping you warm."

Wow, when Clint got into playful sexy mode he was truly lethal.

Finally, she found the packet and made a dive back underneath the cover. "Really? What else could it have possibly been?"

He rolled her beneath him, smoothing her hair back from her face, and pulled the sleeping bag up around them, cocooning them in body heat and sexual energy. "Maybe this." He scattered kisses down the length of her neck, chasing away every last vestige of gooseflesh.

"Oh," she breathed on a sigh of rekindled arousal.

He chuckled low in his throat. "Or this." He dipped his head beneath the sleeping bag and once again, his mouth and his hands found her breasts, his lips teasing, taunting, suckling her until she was thrusting her wetness against his erection.

He emerged from beneath the cover, his eyes glittering in the dim light of the wood stove. "Where are the condoms?"

Her hand unsteady, Tessa fished out one of the foil packets and tore it open. She handed it to him. The way she was shaking, combined with the fact that she had very little experience in the condom department, meant they'd be here all day if she had to put it on.

Luckily, he knew what to do. In a few seconds he was poised between her thighs. He paused and for a moment it was like an impression caught on camera—him etched against the shadows filtering through the cabin, all man and muscle. Evocative. Erotic. She focused on the sensation of him entering her inch by inch and then the thrust as he gained momentum.

"Yes," she said.

She closed her eyes, the better to absorb the feel of him. It was sublime—him deep inside her. It was as if everything stilled inside her and exploded, all at the same time.

They set a rhythm together and with each thrust, each squeeze of her muscles around him, it got better and better when she didn't think it was possible to feel any more intensely.

Her orgasm began to build inside her. She didn't want the lovemaking to end but she also wasn't sure how much tighter she could be wound without totally shattering and coming undone. And then there was no choice to be made, nothing to be done but be swept along in the release that gripped her, shook her and touched her to her core.

CLINT STOOD, THE SHEEN of sweat on him rapidly chilling in the cabin's draft. "Can I get you anything?" he said.

Tessa looked as shell-shocked as he felt which was fairly gratifying. She blinked as if to focus and shifted beneath the sleeping bag.

"A cigarette?" she quipped with a quirky smile. "Just kidding. No, I don't need anything except to lie here for a minute."

"I'll be right back," Clint said.

He covered the short distance from the sleeping bags to the kitchen and made quick work of cleaning himself up. Kobuk raised his head from his corner of the room, looked at Clint, and then lowered his head again, closing his eyes.

Clint returned to Tessa, sliding beneath the cover.

"I want you to know that this is a first. I've never slept with anyone I was working with before."

"I didn't think you had, Clint. I've only known you a few days but you don't seem the type. Plus, if this was standard operating procedure for you, you would've been prepared with a condom."

"There is that," he said with a smile. He was glad she believed him. And he'd felt it was important she know that about him.

"I wanted to make sure you know that this is...I've never...I do a lot of filming and I've never done this before. Condoms aren't part of my travel package. It was my friend's idea of funny before I left."

He would have never asked her but he was pretty damned relieved to hear it. "I appreciate you letting me know."

"Clint?"

"Yes?"

"Would you pass those apple rings that started all of this in the first place? I'm starving." She tugged on her thermal undershirt, not bothering with her bra.

He laughed, snagging the plastic bag of dried fruit. "I'm not sure the apple rings had a whole lot to do with what just happened but here you go."

She grabbed a piece of the dried fruit and bit into it. "Hmm. That's good. I don't know why I never think of buying these at home."

Clint helped himself as well. Now that she mentioned it, he was pretty damn hungry. And they'd both just expended a good bit of energy. He wasn't sure the last time he'd felt this good. Possibly never.

"What do you like to do when you're not filming and editing your videos?"

Her smile held a note of self-consciousness. "I like to cook but since it's just me, I share a lot with my neighbors so they appreciate it. I also dabble in jewelry making—mostly beading. I sell some of it online."

"My grandmother and my aunt are both jewelry makers. I'm not sure what materials they use but they're pretty good at it."

Tessa's face lit up. "Do you think I could meet them? I'd love to take a look at their work and talk about technique."

He wasn't altogether sure it was a good idea but at this point he would've promised her the moon if he thought he could deliver it. "I don't see why not. I'll check when we get back. As long as it's not bingo night it should be fine."

"Do you have a big family?"

Clint laughed, thinking about the crowd that had gathered at his cousin's wedding in September. "Yeah. There's more than just a few of us."

"Any brothers or sisters?"

He felt his face tighten. "No." His father had never remarried. Clint's mother had pretty much broken his father's heart and that was that. His father had disrespected the wishes of his family when he married her.

"How have you reached the ripe old age of, what, thirty or thirty-one without getting hitched?"

He shrugged. "There was no one here I want to marry. There was someone in college. I met her at the University of Alaska. That didn't work out. I think she thought dating a native was an interesting social experiment but long-term just wouldn't work out."

"I see."

He suspected she did, in fact, see. Carrie Turner had broken his heart—ripped it out and stomped on it—and he'd vowed then and there that he was never going to open himself to that kind of pain, ever again.

And he had a few questions of his own for her. "How is it that you're still single? Or are you divorced?"

"No. Never married. I move around a lot. Makes it difficult to form attachments."

"Yeah, long distance doesn't work, does it?" Clint said. This was a good conversation to have. It left absolutely no room for misunderstanding when she left at the end of the week. They definitely shared some chemistry but that was going to be it.

"No, not at all."

Good deal. They were on the same page. Neither

one of them was looking for anything beyond the next couple of days. Glad they had that straightened out.

TESSA HAD NEVER SEEN anything as spectacular as the northern lights. She stood at the cabin's window and watched as ribbons of purple and yellow danced and swirled in the night sky.

"Photos don't do it justice. They certainly don't prepare you for this."

Clint stepped into the space behind her, his very nearness setting off a maelstrom of want inside her. "It's something else, all right. And they're all different. Every time you see a showing, you think it's not like anything you've ever seen before." He placed one hand on her shoulder. "When I was a kid, my grandfather used to tell me it was the spirits in the sky celebrating."

Tess reached up and twined her fingers with his. "I can't imagine what it must have been like to be a kid and see something like this."

His fingers tightened on hers. "It's always amazing." He leaned forward, nuzzling the back of her neck. "And you're pretty amazing."

Sweet heat arrowed through her at the touch of his mouth on the sensitive area. "Clint…"

"Hmm?"

"Make love to me here at the window while we watch the lights."

"There are more condoms?"

Tess turned her head and pressed a kiss to his fingers. "We started out with half a dozen."

His voice was a low, husky murmur against her neck. "Tell me where I can find one."

Tess reached into her front left pocket, pulled out the foil wrapper, and laid it on the counter. "I came prepared."

He wrapped his arms around her from behind and pulled her tight and hard against the length of his body. He slid his hands beneath her shirt and stroked her stomach and sides. She sighed and arched back against him. He continued to touch his way up her body until his hands were on her breasts and all the while he was kissing and nipping at her neck.

There was something incredibly sexy about watching the night sky through the window while Clint turned her on more and more with his touch. The growing ridge of his erection pressed between her buttocks.

"I want you naked," he said. "Will you be too cold? I threw a couple of extra logs on the fire earlier."

"No, I'm actually a little hot." Even though she stood in front of the window, it was warm in the cabin. She supposed that's what happened when you hoped you were going to get naked and threw extra logs on the fire.

His soft laughter danced against her neck. "I think you're about to be hotter."

"I know I'm about to be hotter," he said.

His low laugh turned her on even more. She started to take off her shirt when he stopped her. "No, let me. You just watch the lights."

He was in no rush as he undressed her. There was something terribly erotic about keeping her back to him as he pulled her shirt up and over her head. He slid her bra straps down and pressed a trail of kisses over her shoulders. He stroked his hands over her arms and sides, then released her bra hook. Within seconds her bra was gone and his hands cupped and weighed the fullness of her breasts. He palmed her nipples and then caught them between his fingers, tweaking, tugging, pulling until her breath was coming in short, sharp pants.

"That feels so good."

"You have beautiful breasts and your nipples are so sensitive. I love the way you squirm when I suck on them or play with them."

"I like it too."

"We'll see just how much you like it," he said on a low, gravelly note.

He reached down and unbuttoned and unzipped her jeans. Reaching inside without taking them off, he delved beneath her panties and into the arousal-slicked channel between her thighs. "Oh, you like it."

She glanced down and not only did it feel good but the contrast of his darker skin against her startlingly white skin struck her as the most erotic thing she'd ever seen.

He stroked his finger along her and she mewled in the back of her throat. "Yes, I do."

He slid his finger inside her and she thought she might come unglued right then and there. He added a second finger while his thumb found her clit.

He cupped one of her breasts in his other hand and began to toy with her nipple, setting up the same rhythm as between her thighs.

"If you don't stop, I'm going to..."

"I want you to."

"But I thought—"

"We're going to do that too."

What started out as "okay" became simply a mindless series of "ooohs" as his clever fingers stroked her to an orgasm that took on the hues and colors of the show of lights in the sky.

9

MERRILEE WASN'T SURE exactly how long Bull would continue to ignore her. So far, it had been a few days. She wouldn't have stood for it had there been any malice involved. But this was Bull they were talking about. He wasn't sulking or punishing her, he was simply thinking, trying to come to terms with what he'd thought and what actually was.

Jenna, aka Baby Doll, skipped up to the desk. "Morning, Merry. How's it shaking today?"

It hovered on the tip of Merrilee's tongue to tell Jenna that no one referred to her as Merry, but she simply couldn't take the girl to task. True enough, she more closely resembled a walking talking Barbie doll than any other human being Merrilee had ever encountered, but there was more to Jenna than first met the eye.

The girl might look plastic, but inside she was genuine plastic. She'd been delighted with the mukluks

Merrilee had loaned her yesterday to the point that Merrilee had told her to keep them. You'd have thought she'd awarded Jenna a national treasure.

And even though, according to Teddy, Jenna had wound up painting her own nails because Curl just couldn't get it right, Jenna had thought it was all fun and had found Curl's shop fascinating. Tad certainly didn't deserve Jenna. And more important, she deserved far better than Tad, as had Merrilee. So with all of that water under the bridge, if Jenna wanted to call her Merry, there really was no harm done.

"Just fine, Jenna. And how are you this morning?"

"I'm great! Daddy's a little under the weather this morning. He asked me to tell you he'd like his breakfast in bed."

Merrilee gritted her teeth and reminded herself Tad was a paying customer. "No problem. Would you like your breakfast upstairs as well?"

"Thanks but no thanks. I'm going to head over to Curl's. I told him I'd help him out with some stuff today. No offense, but there's not an awful lot to see and do in your town and I liked hanging out there yesterday."

Merrilee laughed. For a woman like Jenna, who was obviously into shopping and spa visits, "there's not an awful lot to see and do in your town" was a huge understatement. However, she thought it was cool Jenna had enjoyed being over at Curl's. "Okey dokey." Merrilee glanced down at Jenna's feet. "Good girl, I see you're wearing proper Alaskan winter footwear."

Jenna's broad smile filled her face as she lifted one foot as if modeling the fur and skin boots. "Are you kidding? These are tight."

"I thought you said they fit fine."

"No, silly. Tight as in I like 'em."

"Oh...that tight. Okay."

"There's one other little thing. I didn't mention to Daddy I was heading over to Curl's. He's sort of in a snit this morning. If he asks, will you tell him that's where I've gone?"

It was all just too odd for words. If Merrilee and Tad had compounded the mistake of getting married with procreating, Jenna was about the same age their kid would've been. And it was damn strange to have maternal protective instincts toward her husband's fiancée. Nonetheless, Merrilee did.

"Honey, you go on over to Curl's and have a good time. Don't worry about Tad. I'll handle him."

"Thanks, Merry." Jenna threw her arms around Merrilee and gave her an enthusiastic hug. Releasing her new friend, Jenna headed toward the front door. "I don't care what Daddy says about you, I think you're the best."

"Be careful crossing the street, honey. It's icy out there," Merrilee said as Jenna closed the door.

That did it. That sealed the deal. Maybe before,

just to be ornery and thwart Tad, she'd thought about not signing the divorce papers. Now there was no way in Hades she could sign them because as soon as she did, that poor girl would hitch her wagon to Tad's sorry ass and that just wouldn't do.

Someone had to save poor Jenna from making the same mistake Merrilee had at Jenna's age. And as it stood, that someone was Merrilee.

It looked as if she was going to be stuck married to Tad Weatherspoon indefinitely.

CLINT EASED HIS LEGS OVER the edge of the bunk and sat up. Across the small expanse of floor, Tessa lay curled up in her sleeping bag, dead to the world. Actually, her mouth was hanging open and she was gently snoring, her fall of silvery blonde hair draped over the elegant line of her neck. It should've been a little off-putting to see her that way but it wasn't. She looked as gut-wrenchingly sexy as she had last night.

Last night…big mistake. Make that huge mistake. Not only had it been unprofessional as hell, it was just stupid on his part. But he had to admit, being intimate with her had been so damn good. So, he'd been there and done that and it didn't need to happen again. He'd write it off to a moment, make that two moments, of weakness.

He stood, stretching, and avoided looking at her again. Not only did it feel intrusive to watch her as she slept, it really was a subtle form of torture. He so didn't need to go there with her again, but when he looked at her all he could think about was the softness of her skin, her scent, the sound of her voice crying his name on the end of a soft moan as her orgasm rippled through her.

What he wanted to do was climb into bed with her and continue where they'd left off last night. He wanted to slip into the sleeping bag with her and see if she really felt as good, tasted as good as she had last night. But that would simply compound his mistake.

Moving carefully and quietly, he pulled on his socks and boots. The last thing he wanted to do was wake her. Suddenly he was desperate to be out of the room, away from her scent, the soft sound of her breathing, the very temptation of her.

He didn't bother to stoke the fire since Dalton would be arriving mid-morning to pick them up. He shrugged into his jacket. Kobuk waited by the door at rapt attention, obviously ready to get out of the cabin as well. Clint signaled the malamute to lie down again.

He stepped out into the cold morning, then eased the cabin door closed behind him. He didn't anticipate any trouble while he was out, but just in case, Kobuk needed to stay inside with Tessa. He was as effective at guarding as he was at working a sled.

Clint set out in the direction of a stand of birch

trees. He'd promised to bring bark striplings for his aunt and cousin, both avid weavers. The cold and the exercise should clear his mind. God knows, something needed to.

BEFORE SHE EVEN OPENED HER eyes, Tessa knew Clint wasn't in the cabin. She didn't sense him. In fact, not only did she not sense him there, it was as if she felt his absence.

She sat up in her sleeping bag, propped on one arm, and looked around. Other than Kobuk by the door, the cabin was empty. Clint's jacket and boots were gone.

She wasn't ready to face the cabin's chill quite yet. Funny but she really hadn't noticed the chill last night. She settled back on her bunk, snuggling into her sleeping bag. Ouch. Parts of her she hadn't used in a long time were sore.

He wasn't like any man she'd met before. And sex with him had been unlike any other experience. It was as if she'd found something that had been missing all of the other times. Maybe because there was an intensity to him she'd not found in anyone else. It was as if making love had been a deeper, richer experience than she'd ever had before.

Angling carefully over the edge of the bunk, she grabbed her camera and hauled it up. Tessa flipped it on and watched the fantastical lights of the aurora borealis dance across the screen. As she watched the footage, her thoughts turned to Clint. She could feel the press of him against her, the slide of his hands over her breasts, the brush of his warm breath against her neck as he buried himself deep inside her.

Her body grew warm and that increasingly familiar warmth blossomed between her thighs. An ache, a need to have him again, filled her with an intense longing. And as surely as she knew her name, she knew when Clint walked back through that door, he would be all business. If he'd wanted to make love again this morning, she wouldn't have woken up alone in her bunk.

So, she could sit around and wait for what she wasn't going to get or she could take care of things herself. Hadn't she discovered a long time ago that the only person she could really depend on in the end was herself? She might want Clint, but she didn't need him. And that was an important distinction, she noted, as she slid her hand beneath the sleeping bag to satisfy her want.

CLINT CLEARED THE TREES and started across the expanse of frozen river to the cabin. The sun would soon make its brief appearance on the horizon, where it would hover for a few hours until it disappeared once again.

Tessa emerged from behind the cabin, firewood in her arms.

"Morning," he said, his voice carrying across the frozen expanse.

She smiled at him around the load of wood. "Good morning. Out for a morning walk?"

It wasn't nearly as awkward as he'd feared it might be, the whole morning-after thing. "I needed to take care of something. What are you doing?"

"Replacing the firewood."

"You haven't added any to the fire, have you? Dalton will be here to pick us up in an hour or so and the fire needs to be out."

"I do have a little bit of sense. There is a brain cell or two in my gray matter," she said on a teasing note that sounded slightly forced.

He opened the cabin door for her. "Then why are you hauling in wood?"

"There was firewood in the cabin when we arrived. I was sure it had to be restocked before we left so I thought I might as well get on it."

Her rational notion made perfect sense but inexplicably it annoyed him. She was right. The wood needed to be replenished but she was the guest. "That's my job."

She began to unload the wood, adding it to the stack by the door and he automatically helped as well. "Well, I didn't have anything else to do so I thought I'd make myself useful."

He realized he was being an ass for no good reason. "Thanks then."

Glancing around the cabin, he noted all her gear was neatly packed and stacked by her bunk. "Looks like you've got everything in order."

"I try. I told you from the beginning I could pull my own weight out here." She unzipped her jacket and pulled it off, tossing it onto the top of her gear.

"I'm convinced. You don't have to prove anything to me."

Her chin came up and her eyes flashed. This was more than just a conversation about restocking firewood and they both knew it.

"You're absolutely right, Clint. I don't have anything to prove. Not to you. Not to anyone. I brought in firewood because it needed to be done and I wanted to do it. I like the physical activity and I like to be useful. That's just the way I roll. By the way, I saw one of the wolves again this morning. When I came out, he appeared over there." She nodded in the direction of the trees on the opposite side of the frozen bank. "We looked at each other a few minutes and then he turned and left."

The hair on the back of Clint's neck stood up. The wolves were usually much more leery of people. "And he just left?"

"Uh-huh."

"That's strange." His familiarity with the ways of animals and native lore told him it wasn't as much strange as it was significant, but there was a part of him that didn't want to acknowledge the implication.

She stacked the last piece of wood.

"Well, thank you for restocking the wood supply." He sounded as if someone had shoved a stick up his ass but it was the best he could manage.

"You don't owe me any thanks at all. As I said, I did it because I wanted to do it."

Feeling awkward, he knew he'd handled all of this badly but didn't know what to do at this juncture, so he held out his idea of a peace offering.

Shrugging out of his jacket, he pulled the bark strips from the inside pocket. "My aunt and cousins are basket weavers." He held out the thin strips of wood. "I promised them I'd bring some bark back. It's only found in this area, and they prefer to work with it because it's thin and deceptively delicate in appearance, but also very flexible and strong."

The tension that had been between them lifted and she smiled as she took a strip of the silvery white wood and tested it between her fingers. "It's beautiful."

"It is, isn't it?" It wasn't the wood however that seemed so beautiful to him at the moment.

She turned it over, her head cocked to one side, as if studying the piece. "I bet it makes a beautiful woven piece."

Without thinking, simply wanting to see another genuine smile curve her lips and light her eyes, Clint said, "When you check out the beading, you could meet the basket weavers as well."

Her smile was as dazzling as the sun when it topped the horizon. "That would be fantastic."

Fantastic—right. Next to sleeping with her, taking her to his village would possibly be the most stupid move he'd made in a long time.

10

TESSA WAS AMAZED AT how familiar it felt to cross the landing strip and walk into the office once Dalton had them safely back on the ground.

"How was the fishing camp?" Merrilee said by way of greeting. "Did you get some good footage?"

Even though Tessa didn't know her very well, she thought the older woman's smile looked a bit tense. Of course, having a man on your property whom you'd driven across a continent to get away from would make anyone tense.

"I got some great footage of wolves, chickadees and the northern lights. I'm very pleased."

"That's good to hear. We like to keep our visitors happy."

"I can see why you stayed when you got here. It's just beautiful."

"That it is. but it's not for everybody, which is a good thing, because if everybody lived here the rest of us probably wouldn't want to," Merrilee said, winking like a teenager sharing a joke.

Tessa laughed. "Clint had some things to take care of and we're not supposed to head out to the glacier until later this afternoon, so I'm going to explore the town after my shower."

"Do you want a guide? I can snag Teddy from next door."

"No. I'm fine on my own. Thanks though."

"You sure?"

"Positive. I'm used to my own company."

"I tell you what. I'll have a cinnamon roll and a cup of tea ready for you when you come back down. You don't want to go exploring on an empty stomach."

"Sounds like a deal."

Forty minutes later Tessa had scarfed down the best cinnamon roll she'd ever tasted and washed it down with a cup of hot tea. Tad had been nursing what looked like a mixed drink at the bar next door. Tessa had caught a glimpse of Mr. Spray-on Tan when Teddy had brought over the cinnamon roll. She hadn't seen his fiancée next to him but then again, the door had opened and closed fast. Talk about a man who didn't match either of the two women in his life—past or present. She always thought it was interesting to see couples together. Sometimes they looked as if they were meant to be together and other times you were just left shaking your head wondering why and how that pair had come together.

"Be careful. There are ice patches out there," Merrilee called out to Tessa as she headed out the front door, bundled into her parka.

"Will do."

Frigid air whistled down the street and against her skin. She tugged her hood more firmly into place. It was doggone cold, but she found it invigorating.

Merrilee had armed her with an overview of the town. Good Riddance was essentially one major street, appropriately and in good southern tradition named Main Street, lined with stores. Driveways ran perpendicular to Main Street, allowing access to the back of the businesses, or to houses behind them.

She set out for the general store, which catered to the locals as well as stocking a variety of souvenirs for the tourists passing through. Tessa found the day's light very weird. It wasn't exactly dark, but neither was it what you'd call light. It was more along the lines of a twilight—a far cry from Tucson's mostly sunny skies. The difference was neither bad nor good, it was simply different.

A woman, obviously native, passed by her, holding a small child by the hand. She offered Tessa a shy but friendly nod. "Hello," Tessa said in return.

For all she knew, the woman was very likely kin to Nelson and Clint. But then again, perhaps there were different clans and tribes in the area. She'd have to ask. She couldn't help but wonder if there was a woman in Clint's life, even though he didn't strike her as the kind of man to sleep with her if there *was* a woman in his life. The very idea made her faintly sick. No, she'd just be honest. That wasn't a sick feeling, it was called jealousy, plain and simple. She had no right to demand anything, but the idea of him making love to someone else with the same tenderness and passion he'd shared with her last night rocked her to the core. And that wasn't a place she needed to go.

A bell jangled as she walked through the glass-fronted door of the Good Riddance Dry Goods and Emporium. The store looked as if it had been pulled from a movie set. It was a quintessential turn-of-the-century store with slightly dusty shelves, the scent of fresh peppermint candy mingled with a faint mustiness. There were even a few bolts of fabric stacked on a table in the back.

A couple who bore a striking resemblance to Mr. and Mrs. Santa Claus garbed in blue jeans and motorcycle T-shirts greeted her from behind the counter.

"Hi, there," the woman said.

"What can we do you for?" the man seconded.

Tessa introduced herself and her assignment in Good Riddance. In turn the couple introduced themselves as Leo and Nancy Perkins. Within minutes Tessa had the skinny. The Perkinses were transplants from Wisconsin where Nancy had retired from teaching school and Leo had retired from insurance sales.

Their kids and grandchildren came up each summer for a family visit.

"Do you carry locally made products? That's always what interests me most," Tessa said.

"Sure thing," Nancy said. "Over here we've got some necklace carvings, some etchings, and a couple of watercolors by our local artist Henry Mansford."

Almost immediately Tessa's eye was drawn to the necklace carvings. The animal figures were small yet beautifully detailed, showing a high level of craftsmanship. One in particular caught her eye. It was an eagle. Rather than the typical pose with wings outspread in flight, this eagle sat watching from a tree top. The strength, the proud cast of his head, the patient watchfulness—it instantly reminded her of Clint.

"I love this."

"Here, try it on," Nancy said, reaching inside the glass case and bringing it out.

The second it touched her neck, Tessa knew she had to have it. It felt right nestled against her collarbone. Nancy held up a hand mirror for Tessa to take a look.

It was even more striking on, gleaming against her skin. She was thoroughly enchanted. She wasn't a big shopper, but when she found the right piece she knew it and this piece definitely spoke to her. And it would be like taking a piece of Clint back with her when she returned home. "Yes. This has my name written all over it," Tessa said with a satisfied smile.

She browsed a bit more and enjoyed chatting with the Perkinses. Another local came in and she met Donna, a tall, striking blonde who ran the engine repair shop across the street from the medical center.

Another few minutes and Tessa was once again on her way. She was walking past a shop with Curl's written in sloping letters on the front glass. Beneath the name it read, "Serving all of your taxidermy, barbershop, beauty salon and mortuary needs." As if the sign alone wasn't enough to stop her in her tracks, Jenna waved at her from inside the shop.

On impulse, Tessa backed up and opened the door. She could use a cut and how many people could actually say they'd had a taxidermist/barber/mortician style their hair?

CLINT STEELED HIMSELF and pushed open the back door. Kobuk was already curled up in the yard. Clint's grandmother and Aunt Leona, who wasn't technically his aunt but had always been called that, sat at the kitchen table peeling vegetables for stew.

The pungent smell of raw onions pierced the air. Both the women ignored him until he'd closed the door behind him and hung his coat on a peg mounted near the door. Only then did they turn to acknowledge him. "It is my grandson with the restless feet who chooses to join us, Leona."

Clint didn't mention he was her only grandson, restless feet aside. His grandmother, for all her wisdom as head of their clan, wasn't above a touch of drama now and again, more often than not.

"Grandmother. Aunt Leona. How are you today?"

Aunt Leona, nearly as old as his grandmother, went into a recounting of her latest medical problems. They were numerous, her most troubling being a recent bout of gout, as diagnosed by Dr. Skye.

Clint listened with half an ear, murmuring platitudes now and then.

"For goodness' sake, Leona, that's enough," his grandmother finally snapped.

"Hmph," Leona said, getting up from the table.

"Good to see you, Aunt Leona," Clint said to her retreating back as she made her way into the den. This particular scenario always played out the same. Grandmother would snap at her and Leona would retreat to the other room for TV time until they both got over their respective case of mad.

Sure enough, within seconds her shuffling steps ceased only to be replaced with the sound of the television.

"Caribou stew for dinner?" he said.

"Yes, your father killed and dressed one out yesterday. Can you stay for dinner?"

They both knew he couldn't. They also both knew

it was her entrée to discuss Tessa whom she'd surely heard about.

"I can't tonight but maybe you can save some for me," Clint said.

"That's right. You're busy with that white woman." Her disapproval apparent, she made it sound as if he was dating Tessa.

He propped against the counter opposite where she sat at the table. "I'm *busy* doing my job, Grandmother. She hired me to be her guide while she's here."

"Just remember your father and his mistake."

Clint found it unlikely he'd forget since he was the outcome of that "mistake." "I'm not my father," he said, almost by rote as he'd reassured both himself and his grandmother the same thing for years now.

She sent him a sharp-eyed look and merely nodded.

"I'm going to bring her to the village tomorrow. She's interested in the beading and the basket-weaving."

He wasn't asking permission. It was more of a courtesy heads-up that he'd be bringing a stranger to call.

His grandmother's lips tightened but that was the only indication she offered that he'd even spoken. He wasn't surprised. He hadn't expected her to be pleased with his decision to bring Tessa out.

"Have you talked to Ellie lately?" she asked.

Not only had he not talked to Ellie, she hadn't actually crossed his mind since he'd laid eyes on Tessa. And he was damn smart enough not to say that as it would send his grandmother right over the edge. "No, I haven't talked to her in a couple of weeks."

His grandmother shook her head slowly as if she couldn't begin to understand Clint. "She is a good match. A hare is just what an eagle needs. The hare tends to things on the ground so that the eagle may soar."

In his culture, every child was "marked" by an animal upon their birth and that became their totem. It was said that when an animal visited three days in a row following the birth of a child, it marked that child as a member of their animal clan, imbuing the child with the animal characteristics. Clint had been marked by an eagle. Therefore, it was no surprise he had an affinity for finding his way and had become a guide.

"I'm not looking for a mate," he said.

"You don't have to be looking. Often the mate finds you. But you must be smart enough to recognize it."

Immediately Tessa's face came to mind. And that was what scared the hell out of him. Much as when a child was marked by his or her totem, when a man or woman was marked by a mate there was no denying or changing it. He pushed abruptly away from the counter. "And you have to be smart enough to recognize when a mate simply won't work."

"You're bringing this white woman here tomorrow?"

He nodded. "Tomorrow or the day after." He plucked his jacket off the peg and shrugged into it.

"You know she doesn't belong here."

He turned to face her from the doorway. "Grandmother, I'm bringing her for a visit. I'm well aware she doesn't belong here."

As he closed the door behind him, Kobuk stood and trotted over to the truck door. Clint crossed the yard, the truth hitting him like a ton of bricks. The only thing Grandmother knew about Tessa was her skin color, yet already Grandmother didn't like her. All these years he'd deemed his grandmother's attitude as one of protectiveness. In actuality, she was as prejudicial as his mother's parents.

And was he any better?

"WHAT DO YOU MEAN, no?" Beneath his orange spray-on tan, Tad turned red. At least Merrilee thought he was turning red. It was hard to tell with that perpetual orange glow he had going.

She closed the log book and put it away in her desk. She stood. She didn't particularly care for Tad towering over her while she sat. "No means no."

"You've wanted a divorce for twenty-five years and now you're refusing to sign these papers?" He shook the papers clutched in his hand as if she might've been confused as to exactly which ones he meant.

"Uh-huh. That's right." She busied herself sorting through a stack of mail Juliette had brought in on an early morning flight.

Over by the chess table, Jeb and Dwight argued as to which winter had been the coldest in the past ten years. Thank goodness they were nearly deaf and couldn't hear Tad babbling about a divorce.

"But why?"

She didn't bother to even look at him. "I don't owe you an explanation."

"But for twenty-five years—"

She dropped the last letter onto the appropriate pile and cut him off, finally giving him her undivided attention. "You refused to sign. Why did you refuse to sign for so long?" It was rhetorical. She knew exactly why he hadn't signed the divorce decree—because it was what she'd wanted.

"Because I could, Merry." He smiled like the smug bastard he'd always been. "Because I could."

Well, he'd at least spit out half the truth. The other reason was that while he couldn't control whether she left him or not, he *could* control whether she was still married to him.

"There you go, then, Tad. That rolls both ways. I can refuse to sign and I'm exercising that right."

"You're jealous. You're jealous I found someone young and beautiful. You don't want to know that

I'm sporting a wife half your age around town while you're stuck with some old man here in the back of beyond."

She'd tolerated his presence, barely, for the past two days but that did it. He'd crossed a line and she wouldn't have it.

"Let me tell you something, you sorry excuse for a human being. I don't give a flying fig if you're delusional enough to think I'm jealous. Think what you want to think, but let's set the record straight here and now. Bull Swenson pisses more class, more dignity, and more integrity than you have in your entire body. There's no finer man to be found."

A movement in the corner of her eye caught her attention. Bull stood in the doorway between the airstrip and Gus's, his expression unreadable. Tad, in the meantime, stood with his mouth gaping open like a bass on the wrong end of a fishing line.

She'd meant what she said about Bull but she'd had enough of his silent treatment. And Tad...she'd had enough of him long ago.

Disgusted with the lot of them, she turned and marched up the stairs to gather dirty linens. Men! As her Grandmother Danville used to lament, you couldn't live with them, and you couldn't shoot them.

11

"WHAT'D YOU DO TO YOUR hair?" Clint said when Tessa finally showed up at the airstrip center. He wasn't in the best mood after his visit with his grandmother. He hadn't expected it to go well and it hadn't, but nonetheless….

"It's called a haircut," she said, rolling her eyes as if he'd posed a moronic question.

He smiled sheepishly. "I guess that was sort of dumb. I was just surprised. The last time I saw you it was down to your shoulders, but it looks nice. Not that it didn't look nice before but it looks good this way, too."

Okay, it was time to just shut the hell up before he looked any more stupid than he already did. This was not a normal state for him but then again from the moment Tessa Bellingham had climbed out of that plane, pretty much nothing had been normal for him since then.

She touched her hand to her short, spiky hair and smiled. He itched to test it as well. Her hair had felt like a fall of satin against his fingers and hands. What would it feel like now with this shorter style?

"I do like it. It was an impulse. I figured how many people could say they'd had their hair done by a taxidermist/barber/mortician? And if it doesn't turn out, well, it's just hair and it'll grow back. But I think Curl did a good job with it. I'm really pleased." She grinned and he felt all knotted up inside. "And it was a heck of a lot cheaper than what my salon at home charges."

Clint laughed. "Not when you figure in the cost of your airline ticket."

"Well, there is that. Oh, and I got this." She fingered a necklace. "Isn't it great?"

Clint immediately recognized the carved totem on the necklace. His totem. And she was wearing it around her neck, in that hollow that seemed as if it had been custom-made for him to tease his tongue against and kiss. "Very nice," he said.

"I think it's wonderful. The carving is so detailed and I like the way the eagle is sitting at the top of the tree."

"I know the carver. Maybe you'd like to meet him while you're here," he said. It was impossible not to offer to introduce her to people and show her things when she was so eager and curious to absorb everything.

"I would love to. I'm just blown away by this."

"When we go to the village to deliver the bark, we'll stop by then." He knew it would be better not to ask—he shouldn't ask—but he couldn't seem to help himself. "Why the eagle? I would've thought you would have picked a wolf, especially since they came and marked the tent the other day."

"You know, I didn't even think about it. I just saw this and knew it was meant for me." She looked slightly embarrassed as she confessed, "It was as if it spoke to me, as if it was meant to be mine."

An indescribable feeling coursed through him. He nodded.

"Are you okay?" she said. "You look kind of odd."

"I'm fine."

"Am I missing something?"

He laughed. He was making way too much out of something that essentially meant nothing. "Nah. It's just that the eagle is my totem." He explained to her how a particular animal presented itself at birth.

"It actually reminded me of you when I saw it. That's so cool. Hey, do you think…no, never mind."

"What?"

"Well, the wolves came two days in a row, but I guess that's silly because I'm not a baby."

"I already thought about that. It seems as if it has to have some significance but I don't know what it is."

"Is there anyone in your village you could check with?"

Clint noticed she didn't question or doubt the custom and lore of his culture. She treated it with respect and as a given.

"I'll look into it." Unfortunately the person who would know would be his grandmother.

"Thanks. I'd really appreciate it. I can't help but think that wolf was marking me, literally."

A look passed between them, their gazes tangling, and she reached up and stroked her fingers over the carved eagle. Clint swore he could feel her touch reverberate through him.

Clint cleared his throat and checked his watch, breaking the moment. "Dalton should be here at any moment and we'll be heading out to the glacier. You should have an hour and a half, maybe two hours of sunlight to shoot."

"Excellent. I can't wait to see it."

"There are a couple of things we need to go over. The river is frozen, but you can't walk out on it the way we walked on the river we were at yesterday. The glacier makes it unstable. At any point it could crack or move and where you were standing could become a crevasse."

"Seriously?"

"More than seriously. A hiker died last year when that very thing happened."

"Does it happen often?"

"No, but when you're the one it happens to, once is enough."

Dalton sauntered up. "Hey, nice do. I heard you were over at Curl's," he said to Tessa.

"Thanks," she said. "You heard I was there?"

"Honey, news travels like wildfire in Good Riddance, and a new chick in town getting her hair done at Curl's is news." He dropped her a wink and Clint instinctively bristled, feeling incredibly territorial, which was ridiculous. Dalton wasn't coming on to her, that was simply his personality. Plus, Clint knew firsthand just how crazy in love Dalton was with Skye.

Clint needed to seriously get himself together. Tessa seemed to constantly throw him for a loop, whether she was fitting right in with the crowd over at Gus's, learning to set the traces, replenishing firewood, or getting her hair done at Curl's. Nothing she did was quite what he expected. Well, the blunt truth of the matter was he kept expecting her not to fit in, and she kept adapting to Good Riddance and the wilderness without a hitch.

"Are we ready to roll?" Clint said.

"Let's do it," Dalton said with an easy smile.

TESSA STOOD ON THE BANK of the river opposite the massive, towering blue glacial ice and took a moment to simply try to take it all in.

"Does this look like a good spot for you to set up

your equipment?" Clint asked. "Dalton wants me to give him a hand with the plane." The ride out had been a little rocky although Dalton had assured her they were safe. "You'll be okay on your own?"

"No problem. Can I go down to the edge of the water?" It was a fairly steep drop but she thought it was manageable and the closer she could get the happier she'd be.

He hesitated, frowning. "In the summer, when it's calving, it's impossible because the ice chunks send waves crashing over here. And normally I'd say it's a bad idea even with the river frozen, but if you're careful and don't go out on the ice..."

"Awesome!" She was already heading toward the edge.

"Tessa—"

She stopped. He very seldom called her by her name. "Yes?"

"Remember what I told you about the ice. Don't go out there. It's rare but it can happen."

"Sure," she responded automatically, only half listening, already thinking how she'd set the one camera up on a tripod and get some hand-held shots with the other.

"You heard me, right?"

"I heard you." She slung the tripod strap over her shoulder and the two camera cases around her neck.

She approached the edge and started down at an

angle, moving slowly and carefully. Sliding down wouldn't be a big deal but it wouldn't do her equipment any good.

She worked quickly, wanting to maximize the time she could record with the sun out. She set up the tripod and camera and began recording. She pulled out the other camera and walked along the river bank. She zoomed in on the glacier face, which had a fracture running along the front. She stood transfixed. Incredible. Unfortunately her zoom wasn't as powerful as she'd like. If she could just get a little bit closer...

She knew Clint had warned her and she'd listened, but just a few feet? She glanced over her shoulder. Clint and Dalton were buried in the front end of the plane. Just a few feet for a few minutes and she'd come back. And what Clint Sisnuket didn't know wouldn't hurt either one of them.

She edged out on the frozen river bed a few feet. Yep. That was better. Much better. But still...if she could get just a little closer. And she couldn't help but think that Clint was being overly cautious. But then again, that was his job. If he wound up with an injury, he could be sued. What he'd warned her about happened...what, once every twenty years?

The frozen river felt as solid as terra firma beneath her feet. And hadn't he said it was rare? Rare was... well, rare...as in seldom happened. So, what were the odds that today would be the day? And when was she likely to have this opportunity again? Not anytime soon. It was probably fine. It was probably something his insurance stipulated so he couldn't get slapped with some lawsuit.

She moved more confidently across the ice, which didn't actually feel like ice when she was walking on the fresh fallen snow. She brought the view finder up to her eye and was blown away by the magnificent translucent blue ice.

Enchanted, she crossed farther out, moving closer to the towering ice. It was enthralling, beautiful, a once in a lifetime view—it was almost as if she was caught up in a spell.

Before she knew it she was standing right in front of the glacier. Her breath caught in her throat. Truly, truly amazing. She held out a tentative hand and touched it.

And it was at that moment that she felt the ice shift beneath her feet.

CLINT WIPED HIS HAND on the rag and straightened. The carburetor had needed flushing. He glanced over to where Tessa had set her tripod up on the river-bank…and she wasn't there.

She stood right next to the glacier, at the most dangerous point, where the constantly moving, melting glacier met the frozen river. His heart felt like it had literally stopped beating in his chest. He had faced down grizzlies before, but had never known the level of terror that gripped him now.

He took off at a dead run. No. No. No. Nothing could happen to her. He'd told her. He'd warned her.

"Tessaaa," he yelled, her name ripped from his throat.

He slipped and slid across the ice, his only thought to get to her. Meanwhile, she had started back across the ice, her face an even paler shade than usual.

"What in the hell were you thinking? I told you…I warned you," he shouted, enraged. He wanted to shake her until her teeth rattled. He wanted to shake some sense into her. He wanted to sob with relief. Instead, he grabbed her hand in a death grip and pulled her along in double-time.

"I know," she said.

Together they gained the river bank where Dalton waited, concern etched on his face.

Clint released her hand and whirled on Tessa, gripping her shoulders. "Why the hell—"

"You're hurting me," she said.

Dalton grabbed him, "Hey, man, chill. She's fine."

"Goddammit, you know what could've happened," he snapped at Dalton.

Dalton nodded grimly. "Yes. I do know, but it didn't."

Tessa's hands were visibly shaking and her face

remained blanched. "The ice…I felt it move under my feet."

Even though he knew she was safe and standing right before him, Clint felt the same terror he'd known before. Just the thought…

"You could be dead right now. Sometimes the ice flips and there's not a thing anyone can do. By the time we'd have gotten to you, you would've been dead." He grabbed her shoulders again and this time he shook her. "Do you understand that?"

Dalton grabbed Clint and hauled him back. He looked at Tessa and said, "Give us a minute." Pulling Clint aside, he said in a low undertone, "Hey, get a grip. She's a client. You can't go off like that."

Nauseating panic still roiled through him. Dalton was right, he needed to get in control of himself. He never lost his temper. He never reacted like this, like some kind of madman. But then again, he'd never been so damn scared in his life. But she was a client and his behavior was the other side of unprofessional. He'd always prided himself on his level of professionalism.

That was the whole damn problem. She wasn't just a client. He wasn't sure exactly what she was, but somewhere along the line she'd become much more than just another client.

And if nothing else, what had just happened illustrated beyond a shadow of a doubt that Tessa Bellingham didn't belong here.

He nodded grimly at Tessa. "You've got another hour here. Stay. Off. The. River. We'll fly back to Good Riddance and then we'll head out to the village this afternoon."

He'd planned on tomorrow, but they'd make it today. Then she'd see just how much she didn't belong here.

12

"I'M SORRY," TESSA said again, glancing at his taut profile as they pulled out of town in his truck, an older-model Suburban. "I give you my word that for the rest of the trip nothing like that will happen again."

"No, it won't because I won't put you in another situation like that." He stared straight ahead, his grip tight on the steering wheel. "You scared me. I don't think I've ever been that frightened in my life."

There was a rawness to his words, a bleakness that twisted inside her. She'd been alone a long time, relied just on herself. She had friends and neighbors but there was something about his words that seemed to go beyond that. "None of your clients have ever had an accident?"

"Tessa, that wouldn't have been just an accident. You would have been a casualty. When I looked up and saw you standing next to that glacier…"

She reached over, closing the space between them, and placed her hand on his arm. Tension radiated from him, through her. "It was stupid. I just thought… it was so beautiful, but my zoom wasn't getting me close enough. I was just going to go a little way and then it was so tempting to get a little closer." Self-consciously she withdrew her hand.

He nodded, still tense, but not as stiff as before. "I owe you an apology. I've never lost my temper like that. It was unprofessional and it won't happen again."

"You don't need to apologize. I was the one at fault." Tessa turned and looked out the window. Towering spruce lined the road. She thought this was as good a time as any to change the subject. "We're heading…north? Right?"

"Northwest to be exact. If you look up to the right—" he pointed slightly ahead of them "—that turnoff is the drive to Dalton's place, Shadow Lake."

They met an old Land Rover with a winch attached to the front heading into town. The driver, a man with a salt and pepper ponytail, waved and Clint returned the salutation.

The potholes that dotted the road forced Clint to drive fairly slowly, slowly enough for her to catch a glimpse down the road of two cabins tucked at a lake's edge. She liked knowing where Dalton and Skye lived. She liked both of them and it was impossible to be around them and not share in their joy with each other. "It looks nice."

"It's beautiful. The lake is ringed by the mountains so some part of it is always in shadow. That's how it came to be known as Shadow Lake."

Snowflakes began to drift down. "This is beautiful. It's like powdered sugar sifting out of the sky," Tessa said.

"We can pull over if you want to videotape some of it," Clint said.

"That would be great. I didn't know whether or not we were on a particular time line to arrive at your village."

"No. We get there when we get there," he said, pulling the truck off to the side of the road. Tessa pulled out her camera and climbed out into the bracing cold, tugging her hood up over her shorter hair. Funny what a difference it made when you lopped off a few inches of hair. Your head got cool a lot faster.

The road ribboned between the tall evergreens while the snow fell. She set the tripod up and began to shoot the video. Clint stood quietly, watching while she worked. It felt right having him there. It was as if he was part of the moment, part of what made it what it was. She grabbed her other camera and began to shoot footage by hand, scanning the area. On a whim, she panned to where Clint stood by his truck, the quintessential Alaskan native. Just as she'd filmed the town the night before for her own viewing, this would never make it into a video for the world to see. The shot of him by the truck was for her alone.

"Tessa," he said, quietly, a touch of wonder in his voice, "look…at the edge of the trees, there in the bend of the road."

Instinctively she followed his directive without lowering the camera. There, standing statue-still next to one of the evergreens, was a wolf. "Wow. He's big. It's not the same wolf we saw yesterday, is it?"

"No. Even though they can travel a fair distance, we're in another pack's territory now. This is unusual. I occasionally see them a little farther out but I've never seen one on this road."

She knew it was a special moment. She felt it inside her. Something shifted, changed, a recognition of something she couldn't name or label.

She had the sense that if anyone would understand what she was feeling, he would. "It's funny. Wherever I go, I always take a bit of the local culture back with me. Not just with the videos, but personally, as well. But there's something about here that's different. It's as if instead of taking part of this away with me, instead I've found a part of me here. Does that make sense?"

Clint nodded his understanding but he wore a wary expression. "There is a magic here, but there is also a harshness to life that can wear on you after a while. You don't always feel that in just a few days' visit." He hesitated and then said no more.

Something had been on the tip of his tongue. She sensed it had been something important, but she also knew whatever it had been, the moment had passed.

Tessa looked back to where the wolf had been but he had vanished, melting once again back into the wilderness. She'd known before she looked that he would be gone.

She put away her camera and then started packing away the other camera and tripod, feeling vaguely disappointed at Clint's response. It was as if he didn't want her to feel too comfortable here, as if he was continually warning her off connecting with Good Riddance too much. And whatever his problem was, it was just that, his problem. Maybe he was spooked because they'd slept together and he was afraid she was going to attach herself to him.

Well, if the truth be told, she was a little spooked herself. She felt a connection with him she'd never felt with anyone before. And while that was all fine and good, she was going to stick to her rule of not becoming too emotionally involved. It hurt too much to care about someone and then lose them as she'd found with both her parents and her aunt and uncle. It was much better to keep everyone at a reasonable arm's length and that applied to him as well. Actually, that applied to him in particular.

"Ready?" he said as she zipped the tripod case.

"Yes. Thanks for stopping. I got some good stuff

and seeing the wolf was like icing on the cake." She opened the truck door and climbed back in. The cold didn't particularly bother her but the warm cab was definitely a welcome change.

He climbed in, started the truck, and within seconds they were on their way again.

"Anything in particular I should know before we get to your village?" she said.

"No. Is there anything in particular you want to know?"

"Well, I'd prefer not to go in and make a fool of myself or offend anyone, so if you can think of anything along those lines, I'd like to know up front."

Clint laughed. "No. We're pretty much the same as other people. My grandmother sort of runs the show and Nelson's father is our shaman."

"And that means…?" She didn't want to use the term witchdoctor but it was what came to mind.

"The shaman is considered something of a go-between or mediator, if you will, between people and spirits. Shamans mostly work with illness."

"But if Nelson's father is the shaman and Nelson works for Dr. Skye, isn't there a conflict of cultural interest there?"

"Thank goodness not any longer. Except for a few stubborn holdouts, most of us see it as having access to the best of both worlds."

He'd mentioned his grandmother but not his mother or father. "What about your parents?"

Clint's face took on a closed expression. "They're divorced." Tessa kept her mouth shut but she'd been exposed enough to various native cultures that she was pretty sure that had been a big deal. "My father used to work as a guide, now he has a cabin out in the middle of nowhere and pretty much lives as a hermit. When he wants to see people, he comes down to the village, occasionally to Good Riddance."

It didn't escape her notice that he didn't mention his mother. Maybe that was a question for Merrilee later because Tessa had the distinct impression there was something key to his personality that was tied into what he wasn't saying about his mother. And she found she had an almost desperate need to know what made him tick.

"WE'LL STOP BY TO SEE Earl the carver first," Clint said, glancing over at Tessa. Outside it was still snowing, forming a backdrop for her profile. God, but she was beautiful. Every time he looked at her she took his breath away.

"That's good with me," she said with her easy smile that turned him inside out.

It was just damn easier to take Tessa by to see Earl and his carvings before he subjected her to his grandmother. Even though he'd shown his grandmother the proper respect in telling her he was bringing Tessa out, Grandmother hadn't been pleased and he felt sure she was going to offer a frosty reception. It took him a second to recognize he wasn't just opting for the easier path as much as he was following an inherent instinct to protect Tessa from what was likely to be unpleasant.

"Hey," she said, interrupting his thoughts, which was just as well, "is it okay if I bring my camera along?"

"Sure. I think Earl will be thrilled to have you documenting his craft." He made a left and drove down a rutted drive to where Earl's cabin sat in a small clearing.

Earl, somewhere in his late sixties, greeted them on the porch. Within minutes he and Tessa were engrossed in each other. Earl was obviously charmed and Tessa was equally captivated. He loved watching the expressions filter across her face, her spruce-green eyes alight with intelligence and interest. The other thing that spoke to him about her exchange with Earl was the level of respect she showed. There was nothing remotely patronizing, which was what he'd witnessed more times in the past than he'd like to recall when native artists demonstrated their abilities to visitors.

"You made a good choice in the eagle. The eagle is strong. Is there another piece on the table that speaks to you?" Earl asked, indicating the finished carvings on one end of his work table with a sweep of his hand.

"I didn't come for…"

"It is my gift to you," Earl said. "I would consider it a high honor."

Tessa gave Earl one of her sunny smiles and the poor man looked nearly besotted. Clint knew the feeling.

He also knew before she selected it which one she would choose. He was right.

"This one." Without hesitation she selected the wolf. He found it interesting she chose the one of the wolf sitting patiently rather than one of the several in howling poses.

"That is a good choice. Do you want it on a separate necklace or should it share with your eagle?"

"Oh, definitely on the cord with the eagle. I think that would look nice," she said, unfastening her necklace and passing it to Earl.

"It will be good."

Tessa told him about seeing the wolves while he threaded the carving onto the necklace. Earl sent Clint a questioning look. Clint confirmed it.

Earl nodded sagely. "You have been marked by the wolves as one of their own."

Tessa beamed.

"But I thought it was only at birth," Clint said. Tessa's connection to the wolf confounded him, but that shouldn't surprise him because Tessa confounded him in general.

Earl returned the necklace to Tessa. "It is unusual in the extreme but every now and then the animal will sense the soul of one who has just arrived or who has perhaps been reborn." He smiled at Tessa, as if welcoming her. "Such is the case with you."

"I feel extremely honored," she said, and Clint could see the pride shining in her eyes. It was everything he could do not to reach over and hug her, she looked so happy.

She rehooked her necklace and the eagle and wolf sat side-by-side in the hollow of her neck, as if they were facing the world together, there to protect each other.

Clint deliberately looked away, but it didn't matter. The image was one that was forever burned into his brain. And that was just fine as long as it didn't find its way into his heart.

TESSA FELT AS IF SHE WAS floating on a cloud rather than sitting once again in Clint's pickup. Being marked as a wolf was one of the coolest things that had ever happened to her, and she didn't doubt for a second that it had happened for real.

She rubbed her fingers over the two carved figures and a tremor ran through her. She glanced over at Clint. "Thank you for taking me to see Earl. That will be one of the highlights of my trip."

"You're welcome," he said, clearly distracted.

Unbidden, the thought occurred to her that even though she'd seen some incredible natural phenomena such as the northern lights, the wolves, a glacier up-close-and-personal, the highlight remained making love with him in that one-room cabin in front of a wood stove and the northern lights. That, she suspected, would be impossible to top. And if she thought he was already acting gun-shy, that would certainly send him heading for the hills. It was best to keep that little tidbit to herself.

"I think it's still early enough that some of the weavers will still be at the center."

"The center?"

"It's like a small community center. The women get together for basketweaving most afternoons and there are usually a group of beaders. Friday evening, however, is strictly bingo night." He grinned and her heart seemed to flip-flop in her chest. "Don't even think about interrupting bingo night."

She smiled, totally getting where he was coming from. "My great-aunt lived for bingo. She scheduled everything around that and three soap operas."

"Yeah, that's got a familiar ring to it."

"I guess some things are the same no matter where you live." Tessa laughed. "Apparently when it comes to old ladies, it's bingo and soap operas."

"Apparently."

They were driving through what looked like a cutaway of a neighborhood. Small houses, a few bigger than others, were scattered about. A group of children played dodgeball or kickball or some version of one of them. A little girl was playing chase with a husky puppy.

Without even considering it, Tessa pulled out her camera and started shooting. In one of those sublime moments, the puppy and the little girl tumbled to the ground at the same time. The puppy was left standing on top of the child, licking her round cheeks until she was giggling uncontrollably. The entire thing made Tessa smile.

She had steadfastly avoided thinking about children because children meant commitment and commitment meant caring and that was altogether too dangerous, but she couldn't stop the thought that it would be nice to have an apple-cheeked little girl of her own rolling in the snow with a puppy. Unfortunately, the exact image that came to mind was of a native child with Clint Sisnuket's coloring and sensual mouth. She didn't dare glance his way in case he caught a glimpse of her longing. *That* would scare the hell out of him. Who was she kidding? It scared the hell out of her.

They pulled up to a rectangular building. "Here we are. That was Lila's granddaughter you just videotaped. Lila's a basketweaver."

"I'll show her the footage if you point her out. It's definitely grandma material."

She followed him into the building. Inside reminded Tessa of the airstrip office in that the walls, floor, and ceiling were all wooden. An assortment of round and rectangular tables were scattered about the room. A radio played country music in one corner and the sound of women talking and laughing floated through the air. A group of toddlers played in one corner with an assortment of toys. Two babies slept on blankets. The whole place exuded a homey, good energy.

Several of the women waved and called out to Clint but went on with their business. The women ranged in age from what looked like teenagers to great grandmothers. Although a couple of the women shot curious looks her way, she had no doubt they all already knew who she was and why she was here. If nothing else, she'd figured out that news traveled fast in the Alaskan bush.

They approached the basket weaving table. "Afternoon, ladies. I brought the bark I promised." He reached inside his jacket and pulled out the strips. "And this is Tessa Bellingham, who's in Good Riddance shooting nature videos. She wanted to stop by and see the baskets."

Tessa was already fixated on the works of art on the table. She'd thought the bark was lovely when she'd seen it before, but now that she saw it woven... "Hello," she said, glancing around the table and then back to the baskets. "They're beyond lovely." She shook her head in wonderment. "It's like seeing poetry. The lines are so fluid, you can almost see the movement."

Several of the women smiled, nodding, obviously pleased with her assessment. She hadn't, however, said it to garner favor, she'd only spoken the truth. "Would you mind if I watched you work?"

"I could show you how it's done," one of the older women offered.

"I'm not very coordinated but I'd love that if I won't be holding you up."

"Tessa, this is Lila Whitehorse. It was her granddaughter you taped outside," Clint said.

"She's adorable," Tessa said, pulling out her camera. She showed the footage to Lila whose grin nearly split her face when she watched the antics of the little girl and the puppy. All of the women at the table got up and gathered around, eager to see. Tessa enjoyed viewing it again, especially because it made everyone smile and laugh. There was nothing quite like sharing happiness.

Lila looked at Clint. "Bring an extra chair and put it here next to me."

All the other women slid their own seats over a bit to make room. Lila patted the empty spot. "Now, you come sit next to me," she said to Tessa, "and I will show you how to weave with the bark that flows."

A quarter of an hour later Tessa couldn't believe that she, who historically had been all thumbs when it came to any kind of crafting skill outside of beading, seemed to actually have the hang of weaving the beautiful bark. The footage had definitely been an ice-breaker and the women had all made her feel welcome. There was something very soothing and peaceful about the tactile experience of working with the bark, of actually creating something that was not only useful but beautiful. In fact, the camaraderie of the women in general had the same effect on Tessa.

She was in the middle of laughing while Elaine, a woman who appeared to be Tessa's age, recounted the antics of her toddler, when a sudden silence descended on the room except for the radio and the children. Tessa turned to look at the door, which is where everyone else seemed to have fixed their attention.

An older, dark-haired woman and a much younger woman stood just inside the room. The younger woman looked decidedly uncomfortable. Clint stepped forward, "Hello, Grandmother, we were going to stop by and visit on the way out."

His grandmother merely inclined her head in acknowledgment as she crossed the room and approached Tessa's table, the younger woman in tow.

Even though there was a smile on her face, her eyes were flat, which indicated her hostility as far as Tessa was concerned. Tessa stood, since it just seemed the right thing to do.

The other right thing to do was to grab the bull by the horns, so to speak. "Hello, I'm Tessa Bellingham. I've just been enjoying learning the basics of bark weaving." She offered her friendliest, most charming smile.

The other woman's smile didn't reach her eyes, which held a glimmer of malice. "I'm Clint's grandmother and this is Ellie, his fiancée."

13

"SHE'S NOT MY FIANCÉE," Clint said the moment Tessa slammed—and she did *slam*—the truck door closed. He put the truck in gear and headed back toward town.

"That's convenient for you to say now that we're not in front of anyone." She stared steadfastly out the passenger window.

"Tessa, it would've been disrespectful to my grandmother and humiliated Ellie if I had spoken up. I can't call my grandmother a liar in public but every woman in there knows Ellie isn't my fiancée."

"It's really none of my business."

"I'm making it your business. My grandmother's been pushing me and Ellie at each other for a long time now but she and I both know there's nothing there. Intellectually, we should be perfect together but it's just not happening. Didn't you notice how miserable Ellie looked?"

"She did look fairly unhappy," Tessa grudgingly conceded.

"That's an understatement."

"For Pete's sake then, why doesn't she just stand up to your grandmother? Ellie doesn't have to disrespect your grandmother in public but she could have a private conversation and tell her how she feels."

That was easy enough to answer. "Because she's not you." Tessa had been careful not to show his grandmother any disrespect but she had also "handled" her. "You held your own against my grandmother today and that's no easy feat, but Ellie isn't as strong a woman as you are."

Which was probably why he and Ellie had never clicked. Not that Tessa was loud or abrasive, but she possessed a quiet strength and strong will Ellie would never know.

"Your grandmother hated me," she said, with a slight pause, giving him the opportunity to step in and deny it.

"She didn't hate you, but I'm not going to lie and tell you she liked you. She didn't." He regretted how bewildered and hurt she looked and the role he played in that.

"But she just met me. She doesn't even know me. How could she not like me? I'm not used to people disliking me without a reason."

How did he explain it was prejudice, plain and simple? His grandmother had decided before even meeting Tessa that she didn't like her based on her skin and hair color. Instead he told her, "It's complicated and wrong but it's really not about you."

She smiled, her first smile since they got back in the truck, and it was amazing how damn glad he was to see it. "It certainly felt like it was about me, but I don't suppose it could've been since she doesn't even know me."

"I'm sorry she was rude to you. That's not normally the native way."

She shrugged. "I'm pretty tough-skinned. I just wasn't expecting it." She paused as if unsure to continue, but then she did. "And I have to say it was pretty surprising when she announced you were engaged." He knew he would've felt as if he'd been kicked in the gut had the situation been reversed. And she must've thought he was all kinds of a jerk to have made love to her when he was engaged to someone else. She sent an almost-shy smile his way. "I suppose it doesn't matter, but I'm glad you're not engaged."

He'd sworn he wouldn't touch her again but he couldn't seem to help himself. He pulled the truck over to the side of the deserted road, put it in park, and turned to her. He tentatively reached across the space separating them, giving her ample opportunity to object or back away. She did neither.

He cupped her jaw in his hand and she leaned into his touch, rubbing her cheek against his fingers, as if she'd missed him. He'd wanted to do this all day. He'd told himself time and time again it was a bad idea…and it *was* a bad idea…but sometimes there was no getting around it. You just had to go with a bad idea.

"Tessa." He breathed her name on a sigh. He drew her toward him.

"Clint." She came willingly, meeting him halfway across the distance separating them. She cupped her hand behind his neck, burying her fingers in his hair.

His lips found hers and it was like a homecoming. She tasted sweet and tempting and he kissed her with all the longing he'd kept penned inside all day. She handed his passion back to him in equal measure.

They broke apart.

"I've wanted to do that all day," he confessed, tracing his finger along the line of her lower lip.

"Hmm. Me too."

"It's a bad idea," he said.

"Terrible." She kissed him again.

"Awful." He licked her bottom lip.

"Your room or mine tonight?" she said.

"Maybe both."

MERRILEE LOOKED UP AS Bull crossed the floor.

"I heard what you said to Tad today," he said without preamble.

"Which part?"

"The last part. Thank you."

"So you missed the part where I told him I wouldn't divorce him?"

"You what?"

"I'm not divorcing him."

"The hell you're not."

"Nope. Jenna doesn't deserve what she's going to get with Tad. Somebody has to save that girl from herself, and as long as he's married to me, he can't shackle her to him. That would be bigamy, and while he might be a jerk, he doesn't do stuff that's illegal."

"You know how I feel about you being married, and you're going to stay married to rescue someone you just met? Are you sure it isn't that you can't let him go?"

"I know you don't mean what you just said. I despise him. But Jenna could be my daughter, Bull. I can't let that girl make the same mistake I made twenty-five years ago because I'm just not sure she has the emotional fortitude to get away from him… and look how long it's taken me and I'm still not free of him. I can't abandon her to that."

He pulled her into his arms and rested his chin on the top of her head. "You're something else. You know that, Merrilee Danville Weatherspoon? I love you."

She brushed her fingers against the scars marring his neck. "I know you do. And I love you too."

He nodded and there was a sad resignation in his eyes, along with an uncompromising resolution. "I love you, but I won't ask you to marry me again."

He had just firmly tossed the ball into her court. Even with the paperwork signed, getting to a yes on her part would have been hard enough. Now she just couldn't envision a point in the foreseeable future when she would ever get to *would you...?*

Her marriage to Tad aside, it looked like she and Bull were back to where they'd always been which should have been comforting. Why, then, did it feel so dang depressing?

TESSA FOLLOWED CLINT down the stairs the following morning, appreciating all over again the breadth of his shoulders. They'd wound up in her room last night and Tessa was fairly certain Merrilee had a good idea that was the case.

Tessa would be leaving and Clint was the one who had to live here but he seemed okay with Merrilee knowing. For all that there were no secrets in Good Riddance, Tessa knew Merrilee wouldn't be passing along any gossip about them. It just wasn't Merrilee's way.

"Morning," Merrilee called out as they came down the last step.

They returned her greeting. "We're catching breakfast at Gus's and then we'll be heading out to see the eagles."

Eagle viewing was on-schedule for today. Tessa was stoked. They'd drive as far as possible and then sled the rest of the way in to a location where the eagles nested. As Clint had explained in the emails they'd exchanged prior to the trip, it was an unusual opportunity.

Most bald eagles headed to coastal areas in the winter as they required an open body of water that remained unfrozen. Good Riddance was far enough north that most rivers and lakes froze, but Mirror Lake had thermal properties. It remained thawed year round, thus supplying the necessary open body of water and food source for the mighty birds, which were prolific fishers. Clint had assured her she'd get some awesome footage, particularly as the entire area would be rimmed in snow with steam rising off the thermal lake. As with every day that she'd been here, she was looking forward to the trip.

"It should be the perfect day for it," Merrilee said. "What else is on today's schedule?"

"Snowshoeing this afternoon in the Chinna area. There's been lots of moose activity out that way. Lucky's going to hook us up with a lunch to go."

Tessa had to think for a second, she'd met so many people. Oh, yeah. Lucky was Gus's short-order cook who handled the breakfast and lunch demand. A retired military cook, he ran the kitchen with a tight precision. The dinner hour, however, was Gus's responsibility.

"Excellent."

Using the connecting door between the airstrip and the restaurant, they walked into Gus's. About three quarters of the tables were taken.

"Bar or booth?" Clint asked.

"Let's do the bar." There was something about sitting at the long counter where you could see the room and who was coming and going in the mirror over the bar.

Teddy, the pony-tailed, twenty-something blonde who served as Gus's second in command came over with a coffee pot in hand. "High-test for you this morning?" she said with a friendly smile.

"Please."

"Sounds good to me."

Teddy poured two steaming mugs of the fragrant brew.

"Do y'all need a minute or have you already decided on breakfast?"

It was funny but Tessa suspected Merrilee's southern accent had rubbed off on Teddy with her use of "y'all." Tessa and Clint both ordered eggs, toast and hash browns.

Clint's knee brushed against Tessa's and a tremor ran through her. How could he so thoroughly turn her inside out in such a short amount of time? She didn't have that answer. All she knew was that he did.

Teddy had just stepped into the open kitchen and called their order out to Lucky when the airstrip door swung open and Tad and Jenna came in, sitting a few seats down from Tessa and Clint at the bar.

"Have you ever seen an eagle's nest?" Clint asked.

"Never. That's one reason I'm so excited."

"Their nests are the largest of any bird's in North America. The eagles add to the nest every year and some of them can be up to thirteen feet deep and weigh a metric ton."

"Wow!" Before she could respond further, Tad raised his voice at Jenna, making it impossible not to overhear.

"I said you're not going back over there today."

"But I've got two nail jobs coming in. You should see how thrilled they were when they heard I could do it."

"We didn't come all the way to Alaska for you to do nails. We're supposed to be sightseeing."

Jenna wrinkled her nose. "But I don't like snow-mobiling."

"You wanna go dogsledding?"

"Uh-uh. It's too cold. I wanna go do nails at Curl's."

"What? I'm supposed to hang out by myself? I did that yesterday. It doesn't work that way."

"Well, then come over to Curl's with me. It's real interesting. He does taxidermy and hair cutting and when people croak in town, that's where they take them."

"Jesus H. Christ. We travel four thousand miles to hang out with dead animals and dead people."

She waved her hand, laughing. "Nah, nobody's dead right now. Oh, c'mon, Daddy, it'll be fun. I'll give you a manicure while we're there."

"Pedicure, too?"

"You know it."

Tessa sipped at her coffee and exchanged a smile with Clint. She couldn't fathom him signing on for a mani/pedi. Teddy showed up with their breakfast.

An hour and a half later they were following Kobuk and the sled, the wind whipping against her face through scenery she found breathtaking. They had spotted a cabin a couple of rises over and the wind carried the heady scent of woodsmoke. The trail cut through towering evergreens, their boughs heavy with snow. Tessa wasn't sure when she'd ever been happier. It was one of those perfect moments in time.

Clint tapped her on the shoulder, and once he had her attention, he pointed above them. Overhead an eagle circled, checking them out.

They topped a small rise and Tessa gasped at what lay before them. A lake, steam rising off the surface, was surrounded by trees, while snow blanketed the ground. Something inside her responded, a recognition, an acknowledgment. She turned, smiling, toward Clint. With a single command, he stopped Kobuk and the sled.

Even though they'd passed a cabin, their location was remote enough that silence thickened the air.

"What do you think?" he asked, pride evident in his voice.

"I think it's incredibly beautiful."

"I thought you would. It's pretty special out here."

"Yes, it is."

He was pretty special himself. She thought it was a darn good thing Clint Sisnuket belonged in Alaska, because if he wound up in Tucson and she saw much more of him, she'd be in imminent danger of falling in love, and falling in love was the very last thing she wanted to do. Falling in love meant caring, and caring meant opening yourself up to soul-numbing hurt, and she wanted nothing to do with that particular poison.

Pointing in the distance, he said, "There's a nest. Do you see it?"

It took her a second or two to spot it. There it was, an enormous compilation of sticks. "Awesome."

"We'll set you up somewhere near the nest. Will that work?"

"I'm sure it will be fine. All of the other places you've chosen have been great. I think you might have a bit of an artist's eye," she said, teasing him.

He merely grinned and set them in motion once again. An hour later, Kobuk was out of his traces and curled up on the snow. Tessa had set up the tripod on the top of a hill and captured two eagles "fishing" in the steam-blanketed lake. She was beyond pleased with that.

Clint had just flashed her a smile when a terrible sense of foreboding washed over her unlike anything she'd experienced before. She was about to mention it to him when out of nowhere an eagle appeared, which in and of itself wasn't unusual, except this eagle was flying with talons fully extended as if it had spotted an appropriate prey. Clint spotted the bird diving straight at him.

Tessa could only watch in horror as Clint waved his arms and yelled in an attempt to deter the attack without success. What happened next was like a bad dream. The eagle flew into Clint which sent him tumbling down the snow-covered hill. At the bottom of the hill, a cracking sound and his cry reverberated in the silence. Her heart was racing ninety to nothing while she waited for him to stand back up. It took her a few seconds to realize he wasn't going to.

She ran, slipping and sliding down to where he lay still on the snow, bright red blossoming and staining the white beneath him. Blood. He was bleeding from his head. Panic threatened to swamp her. Oh, God. She was out in the middle of nowhere. That crack had been his head.

Did she dare move him? How could she not? She could wait for him to come to, but what if he didn't? His Suburban had a two-way radio but they'd come a long way via sled and she couldn't just leave him here while she went back to radio for help. And what if the eagle came back and attacked him again while he lay injured and defenseless?

The way she saw it, there was only one option. She had to hook Kobuk up to the sled, put Clint onto it and get him back to the truck. Then she had to drive him back to town to Dr. Skye.

She pushed aside her alarm, forcing herself to inhale deep, calming breaths. Exactly how she was going to accomplish all of that she wasn't exactly sure, but she didn't have any choice. Clint's life depended on her figuring it out.

14

THE LIGHT WAS TOO DAMN bright and his head hurt like a son of a bitch. He tried to put his hand up to block the light.

"Easy there, Clint! Hold on just a few more minutes. I'm almost done with the stitches," Dr. Skye Shanahan said, her tone crisp but soothing.

"Stitches?"

"Yeah, you decided to split your head open on a rock when that eagle knocked you down."

It came back to him in snatches. The eagle heading toward him...impact...falling...his head hitting a rock in the snow...and then nothing until now. Small wonder his head was throbbing.

"Almost done...yep, good thing Tessa's level-headed and resourceful."

"Is she okay?" She had to be okay. Anything outside of that wasn't an acceptable option.

"I'm fine," Tessa said from somewhere in the

room, but he couldn't see her. It was amazing the level of comfort simply hearing her voice brought to him.

"You sure you're okay?" he said.

"I'm sure. I'm fine. How do you feel?"

He attempted to laugh. "I've been better."

Dr. Skye jumped into the fray. "She's far too modest to ever tell you, so I'm going to tell you that you owe Tessa. She hooked Kobuk up and loaded you on the sled. Then she got you and the dog into the truck and drove you here to me. As it stands, with a day of rest, you should be fine. You wouldn't have had nearly such a good outcome otherwise."

Nelson moved into Clint's peripheral vision, handing something to Skye.

"Thank you," Clint said in the general direction of Tessa's voice. In all the years he'd been a guide, he'd never been in this situation where a client had been forced to step up and bail him out.

"You would have done the same for me," she said. "Actually you did yesterday at the glacier. And I know how you feel because I've never been so scared in all of my life."

"Okay. Got you all back together again," Skye said.

"I don't feel anything."

"You don't now, but you will. Here, sit up slowly... easy does it."

Clint sat up slowly, swinging his legs over the side

of the table. Tessa sat in a folding chair in the corner, blood on her parka. She'd said she was okay. "That blood's mine, right?"

"Yep. From when I was getting you onto the sled and then into the truck."

He could see the blood had dried by now. "If it doesn't come out, I'll buy you another jacket."

She smiled, shaking her head, and his breath caught in his throat at her sheer loveliness. "No you won't. It adds character, and when someone asks, I've got a good story to tell."

"I'm definitely buying you another one. I don't need to get the reputation as the Alaskan wilderness guide who fell and busted his head open."

Skye snickered as she scrubbed her hands at the corner sink. "It's not particularly macho, is it? Oops. Sorry, guess I shouldn't have said that."

"It's okay. It's part of your charm," Clint said with a smile. "But no, I don't need to get a reputation as a wuss guide."

"Okay, I won't tell the story," Tessa said, her smile fading. "Was that typical eagle behavior?"

"Of course not or I would never have taken you there. I've never known one to do that before." Tessa seemed to have some kind of different energy about her. First there had been the wolf marking the tent, then the eagle attacking him.

"The eagle was sending a message," Nelson said as he moved about the room in his quiet way, throwing away the remnants of items Skye had used to stitch Clint up.

"What kind of message?" Clint asked, not questioning or doubting Nelson's veracity. Nelson's father was the village shaman, and while it didn't always pass down through families, Nelson was a shaman in training. Both men had insights into the spirit and animal world others didn't possess.

"The message was to you, for you, about you, so only you can know the answer to that."

"I'm drawing a blank. Don't you have an inkling or something?"

Nelson slowly shook his head. "No. The message must be filtered through you. It will come to you."

Skye looked at Tessa. "Okay. Get him back over to Merrilee's."

Clint frowned. "No one has to get me anywhere and why would I go back to Merrilee's?"

"You've sustained a head injury. Most likely you'll be fine but you need to take it easy and be observed for the next twenty-four hours. Merrilee's expecting you."

"But—"

Nelson interrupted him. "Bull drove out and picked up the sled—"

"I didn't want to take the time to get it into the truck," Tessa said.

While the sled only weighed about thirty-five pounds, it was a freight sled which meant it was a little bigger and it could be awkward to get into the back of the Suburban if you weren't used to it.

"No worries."

"Bull's got it and he's taking Tessa snowshoeing this afternoon."

"That's not necessary." She was his obligation and he'd take her. Plus, he wanted to spend what time he could with her.

Skye piped up. "It's absolutely necessary. The poor woman doesn't need you passing out because you're an idiot and begin to hemorrhage out on a snowshoe trail in the middle of nowhere." God, he loved the way she made him sound like an invalid and a liability, but there was no arguing with what she'd said. Tessa'd already had to more than rise to an occasion once today.

Skye handed him a bottle. "Your head should feel better in a little bit, but in a couple of hours it will start to hurt again. You might want to take one of these before it gets too bad. It's easier to control pain before it gets bad than trying to dial it back once it's happened. And now, much as I'd love to hang out and chat, Nelson and I have other patients to see."

Clint stood and shrugged into his coat, putting the pill bottle into his pocket. "Thanks, Skye. See you later, Nelson."

"Sure thing." Skye sent Tessa a warm smile. "Why don't you join us for dinner tonight at Gus's? Dalton and I are usually there around six."

"Sounds good."

It didn't escape his attention that the two women had really hit it off. Actually, Tessa had really hit it off with everyone except his grandmother.

He waited until they'd cleared the waiting room and were outside in the cold that bit at his stitches before he gave her accolades. "I'm damn impressed you knew how to harness Kobuk in, then got me on the sled and back to the truck."

Tessa shrugged and grinned at him. "I told you I like to know things. It can come in handy and it did today."

"You're no wilting flower, I'll give you that."

"Hel-lo. I told you that from the beginning, Mr. Sisnuket. You just didn't listen."

No. He'd been too stubborn to hear what she'd been saying.

THAT EVENING, TESSA TRIED not to feel maudlin when she and Clint joined Dalton, Skye and Nelson for dinner at Gus's. This was her last evening in Good Riddance so she should be making the most of it rather than mourning the fact she had to return to Tucson tomorrow. She straightened her back and pasted a smile on her face. There'd be plenty of time for maudlin when she returned home.

"How was the snowshoeing today?" Nelson said.

"It went well. I got some great footage." Bull

was a nice man and she'd enjoyed his company well enough…but she'd missed Clint something fierce. In fact, it was beyond disconcerting just how much she'd missed him. How could she feel this way about a man she'd only met days before?

Everyone around the table nodded but it was Nelson who spoke up. "Many people are under the misconception that we sit up here and hibernate all winter, but there's lots to do and see, even if the days are short."

"And cold," Skye tacked on.

Everyone was laughing when Jenna showed up at their table sans Tad. "Hey. Would you mind if I joined you for dinner?"

An empty chair sat between Nelson and Skye. Dalton spoke up, "Not a bit. Have a seat. Do we need to round another one up for Tad?"

Tessa very churlishly hoped not. She didn't like the man and she didn't want to share her very last evening in Good Riddance in his company.

Jenna slid into the seat and waved a dismissing hand. "He won't be down, unless it's to go to the bar. He's upstairs sulking because I told him I'm not going back with him." She gave an oh-well shrug and smiled around the table at large.

Tessa noted that everyone, probably including herself, looked stunned. "Are you taking a later flight?" she asked.

"Nope. I'm not going back at all. I've decided I'm going to stay."

Skye looked at Jenna, her eyebrows raised. "Stay as in stay here? In Good Riddance?"

"Uh-huh. Here in Good Riddance. I like it here and Curl said I could do nails over at his place. And I thought I'd talk to Gus about maybe helping out here now and again."

"That's great," Skye said, still looking a bit stunned but welcoming nonetheless. "It'll be nice to have another woman in town."

"Hey, you can come by sometime and I'll do your nails. I don't even mind staying over one evening for you since you have a busy schedule."

"That would be fantastic," Skye said. "I don't think I realized how much I missed that."

"You just say when and I'll hook you up with a mani/pedi."

Dalton, Nelson and Clint all chimed in on welcoming her to Good Riddance.

Tessa nodded and smiled but inside her gut was churning. It took her a few seconds to realize that what she felt was envy. Tomorrow she'd get on a plane and return to Tucson, but Jenna got to stay in Good Riddance and be a part of the community and the people sitting around the table.

Dalton whistled under his breath. "Nope. I bet Tad is not a happy camper right now."

"He took it a little worse than I thought he would.

Especially when I told him I wanted to keep the ring."

"That's two wives he's lost to Good Riddance—well, a former wife and a future wife," Clint said, speaking up with a grin. It was apparent there was no love lost for Tad Weatherspoon by anyone around the table.

"Oh, he's not divorced from Merrilee," Jenna said. "She's still his wife."

"The hell you say," Dalton said.

Skye's eyes grew big as saucers. "What?"

"Yeah. Can you believe it? All this time he's refused to give her a divorce just to be a meanie. But now she won't divorce him because she doesn't want me to marry him." She looked around the table giving another one of those hapless shrugs. "I heard him on the phone with his attorney. He thinks I'm an airhead so he didn't even bother to be too quiet while I was blow-drying my hair. I might be an airhead but I'm not deaf. And he called Merrilee an ugly name which I thought was terrible because I think she's a really nice person and everything. So, I decided I didn't want to marry someone like that, plus he lied to me about his age. Can you believe it? I've been wanting something to do other than shop and go to the spa and I like it here, so I'm going to stay."

Tessa, who had only met all of these people a few days ago, felt invested in them nonetheless in a way she'd never felt before. All she could think was how frustrating that must have been for Merrilee to have left a man but still have him control a degree of her life for all of these years.

"Well, that certainly explains why things have been tense between Bull and Merrilee for the past few days," Nelson said.

No one at the table was gossiping. It was clear that everyone was simply concerned.

Dalton smiled, nodding. "Well, that's all about to change. If you're not going to marry him, then Merrilee can sign those papers. And if Tad wants to start balking again, well, he'll be hard-pressed to find a flight out of Good Riddance to get him back where he belongs."

Clint laughed. "Never piss off the man who's in charge of the plane that gets you out of town."

As crazy as it might sound, Tessa knew they'd make it happen. The entire community would back Merrilee and come hell or high water, she'd be a free woman before Tad Weatherspoon went back to Georgia with his tail tucked between his legs.

And that was precisely why she didn't want to get on that plane tomorrow.

15

NO KNOCK PRECEDED HER bedroom door opening. Tessa had known he would come to her.

Silently, they crossed the room to meet in the middle. Clint wrapped his arms around her, enfolding her. She smoothed her hand over his head, giving wide berth to his stitches. "How are you?" she asked.

He brushed aside her concern. "I'm fine." He tangled his hands in her hair, his lips seeking hers.

There was a sweet fire behind his kiss, and in the play of his tongue against hers. He eased her onto the bed and slowly, mouths fusing, hands roaming, they divested each other of their clothes until nothing was left but the slide of skin against skin.

There was no need for extended foreplay. They belonged together. Clint plucked a condom from the bedside table and rolled it on. Spreading her legs for him, Tessa grasped his buttocks, urging him forward.

In one smooth motion, he was inside her and she gasped from the sensation of him filling her.

Nothing had ever felt so right. So good.

He braced his arms beneath her knees and then, leaning forward, grasped her arms, pinning her to the bed. It wasn't a position of aggression, but it was definitely a stance of dominance which left her all the more turned on. She willingly submitted to him. The wolf gave in to the eagle.

Once again, he claimed her as his own with a kiss, this time delving soul-deep inside her, nearly bringing her to tears.

Together, as one, they climbed higher and higher until they soared together, both shattering in each other's arms.

Afterward, they lay together, entwined, Clint still buried deep inside her for what could've been a lifetime. No other man would ever measure up to Clint Sisnuket. She felt as surely marked by him as she'd felt marked by the wolves.

Withdrawing, he excused himself to the other side of the room. Within a few minutes he was back in bed with her, pulling her close, his arms wrapped around her.

Without filtering her thoughts, Tessa spoke from her heart. "Tonight at dinner, I was envious of Jenna." She paused and rolled over, sliding her thigh over his. Then she opened herself, her heart, in a way she'd never imagined she would. "I don't want to leave tomorrow."

CLINT ROLLED TO HIS side and watched the muted light flicker across Tessa's face. He heard her words, but he knew what he knew. This time tomorrow night he would be in his own bed, alone again. And he'd known it from the beginning, known the inevitability. He wanted her to understand at least part of it.

"My mother lives in Montreal," he said without preamble.

She didn't look surprised, she merely nodded. "That's who you lived with in Montreal." It wasn't a question.

"Yes. She came with a documentary film crew. My father, who had been seeing a native woman, was hired as the guide."

"I'm guessing he and your mother fell in love and that didn't go well on any level."

"Uh-uh."

"Were he and the woman from the village engaged?"

"No, but they were just about one step shy of that. Her name was Cassie Chinoowa. And then the documentary film crew arrived. When the time came for the crew to leave, my father was torn. He couldn't go to Montreal. He belonged here but he didn't believe my mother could be happy here and he knew her being accepted by his people would be a huge issue. But he loved her and she swore she'd be happy as long as she was with him. Of course, she didn't deliberately deceive him. I'm sure she meant it at the time."

"That must have really been awkward on lots of different levels."

"Cassie was humiliated and broken-hearted. My grandparents were humiliated because their son betrayed Cassie and he did so with a white woman. It would've probably been better if my father had up and moved to Canada with her...or maybe not. I think it was just ill-fated from the beginning. You can guess the rest."

"How old were you when you and she moved to Montreal?"

"Five. I was as miserable there as she'd been here. My mother's parents weren't happy to have a mixed race grandson in the first place. They'd been as against the marriage as my father's parents. And to add insult to injury, I looked totally native."

"Yes, you do. Let me guess that your mother is blonde."

Clint nodded. "Scandinavian ancestry. That's where I got my height. I came back when I was seven."

"Did either of them ever remarry?"

"No. I think they really loved each other, probably still do. She just couldn't live here and he couldn't live there. If you consider Good Riddance's population…well, it's obviously not the place for a lot of people."

"Do you see her often?"

"When I was younger she'd come out and visit in the summers but then I started spending my summers as a guide and it was very awkward between my mother and my father's family so we saw each other less and less. She came to my college graduation and then I saw her a couple of years ago."

"Now I know why your grandmother didn't like me. It doesn't make it right, but I at least understand now. Her attitude makes a little more sense."

"She doesn't want to see me hurt the way my father was."

"It might also have something to do with the fact that she felt humiliated."

"I'm sure that plays a role in her hostility."

"It's not hostility. It's called prejudice, the same as it was when you went to Montreal and your mother's family treated you shabbily because of your native heritage. And if she treated your mother the way she treated me, I can understand why it was difficult for your mom to stick it out."

"Funny, I never thought of it from that perspective." All this time he'd simply seen it as his mother not having what it took to adapt to life in the village, not that his grandmother might have made it as impossible for his mother as her parents had made it for him.

"You know your grandmother isn't going to give up until you've married a native woman." She hesitated and then continued, "Unless you stand up to her." Once again she hesitated as if unsure of the boundaries. "You know, Clint, you don't have to atone for your father. His choices were his choices."

"Our whole family paid for his choices."

"You were a kid, so yes, you were caught up in something outside of your control, but everyone else… they're adults and how they react and respond to different situations is up to them and their choice."

"But you understand—"

"What I understand is you're determined not to be your father. I get that. But are you so caught up in not being him that you've lost sight of who you are?"

Clint didn't have an answer for her. He wanted to unequivocally say no, but he couldn't. He also wished he could tell her not to go tomorrow, but that didn't seem possible either.

TESSA ROLLED THE LAST of her clothes into her suitcase and looked around her room at the bed-and-breakfast to make sure she wasn't leaving anything behind.

It was crazy but leaving Good Riddance was turning out to be one of the hardest things Tessa had ever done. And if leaving Good Riddance was difficult, saying goodbye to Clint Sisnuket was wrenching. Last night, she'd almost invited him to Tucson but she couldn't see him coming and even if he were willing, it was a bad idea. She'd confessed she didn't want to leave, perhaps looking for some validation that she belonged here, with him. However, he'd made it abundantly clear they didn't have a future based on the history with his parents and his grandmother's attitude. And Clint wasn't a casual kind of guy—she'd known it from the moment she'd met him.

Severing ties before she became any more attached seemed like the best plan. And somehow, some way, she had slipped up and become attached. Terribly attached. In fact, it seemed to her that her heart was breaking. But it was better to end it now than to get deeper and deeper in and more invested. She'd had enough heartache to last her a lifetime.

A knock sounded on her door. "Who is it?"

As if conjured up by her thoughts, Clint answered. "It's me."

He'd returned to his room this morning before the rest of the bed and breakfast guests were up and about. "Come on in."

He entered, closing the door behind him. "I thought I'd say goodbye privately."

Things felt unutterably awkward between them. When they'd first met there had been excitement tinged with reluctance and almost hostility, but this... this was painfully awkward.

"Okay," she said, at a loss for anything to add to that.

He shifted from one foot to the other. "What are you doing for Thanksgiving?"

His question simply irritated her. "Right now I plan to be editing footage I shot here." She zipped her case closed. There was a finality about it that wasn't lost on her.

"That's not what I meant. I meant who will you spend the day with? Some friends? Some other family members?"

What difference did it make to him? "I usually order take-out from someplace and work."

"Take-out?" A disapproving frown drew his dark eyebrows together. "Alone?"

She wanted to slap him. How dare he give an implied criticism of her choices? She'd offered to be part of his life last night and he'd passed. "There's nothing wrong with that. I'm not comfortable making myself a part of someone else's celebration." Her life was vastly different from his, where he was part of a clan and a larger community. "Besides, you forget I've been marked by the wolves so being alone is right in keeping with my totem."

"No." His dark eyes held her gaze. "Wolves aren't solitary creatures. They live and travel in packs. A wolf totem indicates loyalty and intuition as well as spirit."

Tessa wasn't sure why, but that made her even more unhappy and disquieted. She squared her shoulders. What was her problem? She'd come here alone and she was going home alone. And whatever had happened in between was just that, a lull, an interlude. To have wanted anything more was not only foolish, but dangerous.

"Thanks for showing me such great sights. I got some awesome footage and the videos should turn out well."

She held out her hand. Part of her wanted to howl at the notion of shaking his hand, the other part of her thought she might shatter if he actually hugged her.

He shook her hand. "Tessa…"

"Take care, Clint." She dropped his hand.

He hesitated and then said, "You take care, as well."

She'd be alone just as she'd been and just as she was meant to be.

MERRILEE LOOKED AT Tad and then glanced over her shoulder to Dalton. "Dalton, did you tell me that the plane's at its weight limit and you're not going to be able to get another passenger on today?"

Dalton shrugged. "Yep. And I'm booked up tomorrow too."

"Then I guess you'll have to line another plane up for me," Tad said.

Just as Merrilee had anticipated, Tad was nice and pissed about Jenna's decision to stay. Subsequently, he was now refusing, once again, to sign the papers.

Surely, sooner than later, since it had already been twenty-five years, the papers would be signed and she'd no longer be married to this poor excuse of a human being.

"That's going to be difficult. Everybody's pretty tied up now, pre-holiday rush and such," Merrilee said.

"I know what you're trying to do."

He could sign or his sorry hide would be stuck here, where everyone knew Jenna had dumped him and Merrilee had moved across the continent to get away from him. Merrilee shrugged. "I'm just saying you could be here for a while."

Tad glanced from Merrilee to Dalton and Bull who had come in mid-discussion. Merrilee saw it in his face the minute Tad decided. "Fine. I'll sign the damn papers." He looked at Dalton, his nostrils flaring. Tad snatched up a pen, and within three seconds, the papers bore his signature. He tossed the pen onto the desk and glared at Dalton. "Now do you think you can adjust the weight limits on your plane?"

Dalton grinned. "I'll see what I can do about shifting some cargo deliveries to a different day."

Merrilee felt as if a gorilla—make that jackass—was off her back. Bull turned silently and left the room. But she wasn't sure if she and Bull were ever going to be right again.

16

CLINT WALKED INTO GUS'S. The lunchtime crowd was fairly heavy. Donna laid some cash on the bar and stood, leaving her seat next to Nelson empty. Clint nodded a greeting to Donna and slid into the vacant spot.

"How's it going, Nelson?"

"No complaints. You?"

Teddy approached on the other side of the bar. "Hey, Clint. What'll it be today?"

"Moose burger, fries and a tea."

"Sure thing."

Teddy headed for the open kitchen and Nelson shot him a sidelong glance. "You ever figure out that eagle message?"

"Nope."

"Have you tried?"

"I've been…distracted." He'd been damn miserable is what he'd been. It was as if he'd lost a part of himself when Tessa had climbed on-board and flown out with Dalton. He couldn't count the number of times he'd wondered what she was doing and how she was doing. He'd been tempted to drop her an email but he never did. He'd never felt this way before.

He'd kept up his same routine, waiting for things to return to normal, waiting to find pleasure and joy in the wilderness that had always spoken to him. Now, however, it had grown silent.

"You'll have to clear your head before you can hear what you're meant to hear."

"Maybe there is no message. Maybe it was just a freak accident."

Nelson shook his head. "There's a message. But you have to open yourself to it."

Teddy delivered Clint's food and Nelson pushed away from the bar. "Sorry, got to run." Nelson clapped Clint on the back. "Take it easy."

Clint ate about a third of his meal but didn't really taste it. He got up and spoke to a couple of people on his way out, whistling for Kobuk when he stepped outside. The dog joined him and jumped into the truck ahead of him. He cranked the engine, then headed toward home. Everything seemed meaningless. He couldn't think. He couldn't eat. He couldn't sleep.

He was driving near the spot where the wolf had appeared that day when it hit him like a glacier calving and sending waves crashing to the shore.

He needed…Tessa. The eagle had knocked him down, literally sending him sprawling and cracking his head, telling him to quit listening to his head and pay attention to his heart instead. He had been so damn busy trying to prove to Tessa that she didn't belong, didn't fit here, that he'd refused to see she'd been marked and she'd marked him.

For as much noise as he'd had in his head and as stubborn as he'd been, it was now all abundantly clear. A wolf and an eagle were a perfect complement to each other. They were both strong and loyal, and while the wolf ranged the earth, the eagle ruled the sky. The two dominions meshed in perfect synchronicity.

It was as if when the scales fell from his eyes, all was revealed. He knew what he had to do. He drove out to the village and parked in his grandmother's yard.

He found his grandmother alone in the kitchen, the TV going in the next room. Apparently she and Aunt Leona had already had words for the day and Aunt Leona was working off her mad.

"Grandmother, I have something to tell you."

"It's a mistake." She cut to the chase, her eyes knowing, reading his heart and his intention.

He had listened with his head for so long, but now his heart stood strong. "No, it isn't. She isn't. She belongs here as surely as you and I do." He relayed the incident of the wolf marking Tessa. "It doesn't matter what color her skin is, the wolf recognized her soul as one of its own."

The old woman tightened her lips in stubborn disapproval.

She had raised him, stepping in for his mother. Clint loved her, he respected her, but he would not live his life by her dictates. "I'm going for her and I hope she'll come back with me. If I am lucky enough that she returns with me, you have a choice. You can either welcome her as a granddaughter in a way you never welcomed my mother as a daughter—"

"She was no daughter of mine."

It was funny, you accepted circumstances of your life for years without question. Things were as they were and you simply moved forward. Now, for the first time in his life, he wondered, and so he asked his grandmother, "Did you ever lay down the rug and pass along the lantern for my mother?"

It was a long-standing tradition in their clan. In a harsh and cold climate, warmth and fire meant the difference between life and death. In the days of old, the rug was sewn together with either bear or seal skins, and it offered protection against the cold ground. The lantern had traditionally been whale oil and was kept going so that fires could be maintained, ensuring the family didn't freeze to death. When a man married, his mother welcomed the bride into the family by laying down the rug and passing along a lantern, thus ensuring the new couple would have a chance at a good life. Over the years, the rugs were no longer real animal skins and commercial lanterns had replaced the whale oil lamps of old, but the symbolism was still the same. It was one of acceptance and the wish to live and prosper together.

His grandmother's black eyes bore into his, proud and unyielding. "She was not my daughter."

"She could have been." Sadness and more than a hint of anger tinged him. He had a new insight into what life here must have been like under his grandmother's cold, harsh disapproval. But the past was done. He raised his head, returning her stare. "You can lay down the blanket and pass the lantern to Tessa or I can move out of the village and into town. And if she doesn't want to live here, I'll move to Tucson."

Unrelenting, unyielding, she narrowed her eyes at him. "You would put this woman before your own people? Your own land?"

He didn't hesitate, yet he let the silence stretch between them. Once he spoke, there would be no going back. "Yes, I would."

Cunning flashed in her eyes. "It is your father and mother all over again, I—"

He interrupted her. No more. "I am not my father and Tessa is not like my mother." Actually, had his father truly put his mother first, they might have stayed together. "We are each our own selves. Tessa is strong and resourceful."

His grandmother looked positively grim. "What about Ellie?"

He shrugged. Ellie was the least of the matter. Not because he was callous and unfeeling but because the woman wasn't interested in Clint in the least. "Ellie is no more interested in me than I am in her."

"She's never told me that."

"And she won't because she's not as strong as Tessa." He stood tall and resolute. "You have a choice to make, Grandmother, because if Tessa will have me, I'm hers."

TESSA STOOD IN HER bedroom window overlooking the front courtyard, unable to sleep, feeling like a stranger in her own home. Mainly because she didn't want to be here, and this wasn't where she belonged anymore. She wanted to be back in Good Riddance, but mostly she wanted to be with Clint. It didn't matter whether she'd wanted to love him or whether she'd allowed herself to love him…she simply did.

In the distance, a coyote howled, a different sound from the howl of the wolf. It reminded her of the beliefs of Clint's people, and suddenly she knew the truth. She and Clint had marked each other. It was indisputable. Undeniable. She wouldn't give up on him…on them.

She had wanted, needed validation from him, but she realized that wasn't the way it worked. If she had learned nothing else from losing her parents and then her aunt and uncle, it was that life was uncertain and every day should be seized and lived to the fullest. She could pursue her life list but not the man she loved or the place she belonged? No.

The moon cast a swath of light across her floor and she edged her toe in and out of the light, thinking. This house was paid for. It had been for years, long before her aunt and uncle had died. She could either sell it or rent it and use that money to buy a place in Good Riddance. She could work from there. It would just mean a little extra planning to commute out of Anchorage.

She stepped into the moonlight and looked out into the front yard. At that moment she realized she didn't want to continue traveling the globe, wandering as a child of the world. She'd found where she belonged and now it was up to the next person to step in as an ambient videographer. Part of what she was meant to do was obviously bring videos to people. Now she'd simply do that on a much smaller scale. She'd open a video store and screening room.

She crossed the room to her bed and slid back between the sheets. Lying on her side, she stroked the eagle carving on her necklace. She fell asleep thinking of Clint Sisnuket.

THE TAXI PULLED UP IN front of a stucco single-level house topped with a red-tile roof. Clint wiped his palms down the front of his jeans. He'd rehearsed what he wanted to say to Tessa innumerable times but he was still nervous.

He hadn't called or emailed. She'd given him a chance to ask her to stay and he'd given her some lame story about his parents. He'd come to present his case in person.

"You getting out, buddy?" the driver said.

"Yeah. Here you go." He handed over the fare and a tip.

"Thanks," said the cabbie. "You want me to wait?"

Clint was going into this optimistically. "Nope."

Slinging his overnight bag over his shoulder, he climbed out and approached the front door.

He'd gained an hour on the flight from Anchorage to Tucson. It was early morning and he figured he would catch her at home. If not, he'd simply wait. He knocked on the door.

It took a minute or two but then the lock turned on the other side and she stood there, wearing a pair of green pajamas, her eagle/wolf necklace and a shocked expression.

"Clint?"

"May I come in?"

"Of course. Certainly." She stepped aside and he walked past her into a terra cotta tiled foyer.

She closed the door behind him and all he could do was stare at her, drinking in the sight of her, inhaling her scent.

"I've missed you," he said, hands by his side.

She nodded, a wariness shadowing her eyes. "I've missed you as well."

In that moment, all his nervousness vanished. This was right. They belonged together. He spoke the words he'd come to say. "I love you. I believe you love me as well. Other people might think this is too soon but we've marked each other. All these years I didn't truly understand that my father required too much of my mother and wasn't willing to meet her half way. If you want to we'll live in Good Riddance. If that doesn't work for you, I'll move to Tucson."

She stood, tense, as if she might turn and flee at any moment. "But you love Good Riddance. You love Alaska."

"I love you more. Without you, I no longer find the joy in my land I once did."

"You would give up Alaska for me?"

"Yes."

She flung herself at him, throwing her arms around him. "Oh, Clint!"

He held her, reveling in the feel of her curves pressed against him, showering her face and neck with kisses. His lips found hers and he claimed her as his own.

When they broke apart, she lightly touched the stitches on his scalp. "You're okay?"

Even though he knew it had been a message and an important one he'd needed to receive, he still found that whole incident slightly embarrassing. "I'm fine."

"You must have gotten up incredibly early to be here now."

He laughed, remembering Dalton's grumbling at having to fly Clint out so early. "Yeah, me and Dalton both. He wasn't a particularly happy camper but he's a man who understands what it's like to be in love."

Tessa beamed, a sly look creeping into her eyes. "You must be exhausted. You probably need to rest, have a good nap."

He knew exactly where she was going with this. "Maybe you could show me your bedroom."

She took him by the hand. "Right this way, Mr. Sisnuket."

Epilogue

"You happy?" Clint's warm breath stirred against Tessa's hair as he leaned forward and asked the question in the middle of Good Riddance's Thanksgiving celebration.

"Never happier...except when you showed up on my doorstep," she said. It was wonderful, crazy chaos at its finest. The door between Gus's and the airstrip had been propped open for people to move back and forth. Tables of every size and shape had been brought into the airstrip office. Nearly every dish you could imagine was laid out for the potluck event. And everything smelled wonderful.

"I think your eggs are going to be a hit," Clint said, tightening his arm around her, boldly claiming her as his own to everyone in the room.

"I hope so. That was really generous of Gus to share her kitchen."

When Clint had first mentioned her coming back

to Good Riddance with him for Thanksgiving, she'd protested. She had too much to do to get her affairs in order in Tucson for her move, but the truth of the matter was she'd wanted to be part of that celebration from the moment she'd heard about it. So, they'd flown in the day before and Gus had graciously allowed Tessa free range of her kitchen that evening to make deviled eggs as her contribution.

"Hey, it's so good to see you again," Skye said, giving Tessa a hug. "Welcome back. I had a feeling you'd be returning."

Tessa laughed. "You did?"

"Oh, yeah." She glanced between Tessa and Clint, smiling. "Having just been in your shoes not too long ago."

"Where's Dalton?" Clint asked.

"He and Bull are over at Gus's setting up the karaoke for after everyone eats. Hey, there's Curl. If you'll excuse me, I need to check and see if that cough medicine I gave him is working for him."

Skye headed toward Curl and Tessa touched Clint lightly on his arm. "It's fine if you want to go find them."

"I'll wait," he said, his dark eyes solemn beneath his smile.

She knew what he was doing and loved him all the more for it, but it wasn't necessary. "It's okay, really."

Clint's grandmother would arrive sooner or later.

She never missed the Thanksgiving feast. The unknown factor was how she'd respond to Tessa's presence.

"I'm staying right here for now because next to you is where I want to be."

It wasn't necessary but Tessa was glad of his quiet strength next to her. Merrilee had just bustled over, wearing one of her signature flannel shirts trimmed in lace, a smile on her face. "How do you like our little get-together so far?"

"I love it." Tessa noticed a faint shadowing beneath the other woman's eyes. Tad might be gone and her divorce might be done, but Tessa feared things were still awry between Merrilee and Bull.

Something, or someone, caught Merrilee's attention over Tessa's shoulder. Merrilee grasped her hand, giving it a reassuring squeeze, while she looked at Clint. "She's here."

Clint's arm tightened around Tessa and she knew without turning that his grandmother had arrived. Slowly, as if someone were adjusting the volume down on a television, the conversation in the room grew quieter until the only noise was that of the children chattering.

As one, Clint and Tessa turned. His grandmother, unsmiling, bridged the final few feet, until she stood before them.

"You're back," she said to Tessa, without preamble.

There was no hostility, nor was there welcome in her words or expression.

"I am." Tessa responded in the same vein.

"You are of the wolf?"

"I am."

She narrowed her dark eyes at Tessa. "You love my grandson?"

"I do." Her words felt as if they carried more weight than a vow in a church ceremony.

The harsh angles on the weathered face before Tessa softened slightly. "There is much of our culture you don't know."

"There is much I want to learn."

Even the children quieted and it was as if everyone in the room held their collective breaths.

The old woman stared hard at Tessa, as if seeking passage to her very soul. The silence seemed to stretch on forever and back through generations as well.

"Then there is much I can teach you. I will lay my rug down for you and pass along the lantern... Granddaughter." She nodded as if there was nothing more to be said, and really there wasn't. She had just accepted Tessa as a member of the Sisnuket family.

Tessa nodded in return. "I look forward to it."

As if a wave of relief had passed through the room, conversations started again.

"Thank you," Clint said quietly to his grandmother.

The stern visage softened. "I want you to be happy, Grandson."

"I am. We are."

Tessa felt as if she had come full circle on a journey she hadn't realized she had even embarked on years ago. They would have the ups and downs, their trials and tribulations that faced any couple, but together, the eagle and wolf would find happiness together.

See below for a sneak peek from our classic
Harlequin® Romance® line.

Introducing DADDY BY CHRISTMAS by Patricia Thayer.

MIA caught sight of Jarrett when he walked into the open lobby. It was hard not to notice the man. In a charcoal business suit with a crisp white shirt and striped tie covered by a dark trench coat, he looked more Wall Street than small-town Colorado.

Mia couldn't blame him for keeping his distance. He was probably tired of taking care of her.

Besides, why would a man like Jarrett McKane be interested in her? Why would he want to take on a woman expecting a baby? Yet he'd done so many things for her. He'd been there when she'd needed him most. How could she not care about a man like that?

Heart pounding in her ears, she walked up behind him. Jarrett turned to face her. "Did you get enough sleep last night?"

"Yes, thanks to you," she said, wondering if he'd thought about their kiss. Her gaze went to his mouth, then she quickly glanced away. "And thank you for not bringing up my meltdown."

Jarrett couldn't stop looking at Mia. Blue was definitely her color, bringing out the richness of her eyes.

"What meltdown?" he said, trying hard to focus on what she was saying. "You were just exhausted from lack of sleep and worried about your baby."

He couldn't help remembering how, during the night, he'd kept going in to watch her sleep. How strange was that? "I hope you got enough rest."

She nodded. "Plenty. And you're a good neighbor for

HREXP1210

coming to my rescue."

He tensed. Neighbor? *What neighbor kisses you like I did?* "That's me, just the full-service landlord," he said, trying to keep the sarcasm out of his voice. He started to leave, but she put her hand on his arm.

"Jarrett, what I meant was you went beyond helping me." Her eyes searched his face. "I've asked far too much of you."

"Did you hear me complain?"

She shook her head. "You should. I feel like I've taken advantage."

"Like I said, I haven't minded."

"And I'm grateful for everything…"

Grasping her hand on his arm, Jarrett leaned forward. The memory of last night's kiss had him aching for another. "I didn't do it for your gratitude, Mia."

Gorgeous tycoon Jarrett McKane has never believed in Christmas—but he can't help being drawn to soon-to-be-mom Mia Saunders! Christmases past were spent alone…and now Jarrett may just have a fairy-tale ending for all his Christmases future!

Available December 2010, only from Harlequin® Romance®.

HARLEQUIN®

A Romance

FOR EVERY MOOD™

Spotlight on

Classic

Quintessential, modern love stories
that are romance at its finest.

See the next page
to enjoy a sneak peek from
the Harlequin® Romance series.